"I haven't come to make love to you."

Leon mocked Roselle softly. "Then why have you come?" he asked. "Not just to tell me you're starting divorce proceedings. You could have done that through a lawyer."

"It seemed more civilized to see you first and discuss it reasonably," she said.

"Ha!" He laughed as he picked her up and carried her across the room.

She began to pummel him with her fists. "Leon, I don't love you anymore. Anything you do now will be against my will...."

"You've lied to me before," he said, as he put her down on the four-poster bed.

"But I'm not lying. I don't love you."

"What is love?" he jeered. "Mostly wanting. You still want me—that's why you came here."

"It isn't," she argued. But her voice, shaken with passion, made a mockery of her words....

Other titles by

FLORA KIDD
IN HARLEQUIN PRESENTS

Other titles by

FLORA KIDD
IN HARLEQUIN ROMANCES

Many of these titles, and other titles in the Harlequin
Romance series, are available at your local
bookseller. For a free catalogue listing all available
Harlequin Presents and Harlequin Romances, send
your name and address to:

HARLEQUIN READER SERVICE,
M.P.O. Box 707,
Niagara Falls, N.Y. 14302

Canadian address:
Stratford, Ontario, Canada N5A 6W2

FLORA KIDD

the arranged marriage

Harlequin Books

TORONTO • LONDON • NEW YORK • AMSTERDAM
SYDNEY • HAMBURG • PARIS • STOCKHOLM

Harlequin Presents edition published July 1980
ISBN 0-373-10370-0

Original hardcover edition published in 1980
by Mills & Boon Limited

CHAPTER ONE

THE restaurant was one of the oldest and most famous eating places in Paris. Situated on the Quai de la Tournelle, it had wide convex windows draped with fine grey net framed by folds of crimson velvet. The same rich material covered the elegant dining chairs which were set about round tables gleaming with white damask cloths, crimson-edged dishes and fine sparkling glassware.

At one of the tables near a window overlooking the smooth sky-reflecting waters of the Seine and the sun-gilded twin towers and dark tapering spire of Notre Dame two people were lunching tête-à-tête. Three waiters dressed in traditional black and white hovered discreetly until the wine had been poured and tasted, then withdrew silently.

Roselle Stanson picked up and broke a crisp French roll in half. She spread thick yellow butter on the white bread which burst like foam out of the golden crust. Between her small white teeth the crust crackled as she bit it with obvious enjoyment.

Small and so thin that the delicate bones in her

neck gleamed like ivory through her skin whenever she turned her head, she looked as if she ate no more than a tiny bird, but she attacked the pressed duck for which the restaurant was renowned with all the zest of a person with a large appetite.

Sitting opposite to her Adrian Corwell watched her, a smile of indulgent affection warming his pale slightly protuberant blue eyes.

'I'm always amazed by the way you can eat so heartily and remain so sylph-like and delicate-looking,' he said admiringly.

Roselle laid down her knife and fork. She looked up at him, her large green almond-shaped eyes set beneath arching dark eyebrows widening expressively.

'As a ballet dancer I use a great deal of nervous and physical energy which has to be replaced by good food. Like an athlete, I burn up everything I eat,' she replied, reaching out a slender hand for her wine-glass. She sipped from it. 'Mmm, champagne!' she murmured appreciatively, and her wide mouth tilted upwards at the corner in a smile. 'I get the impression we're celebrating something, coming to this wonderful place for lunch and drinking champagne.'

'We are,' he replied, raising his own glass in a toast. 'We're celebrating your debut as *Giselle*. To you, Roselle darling. You were wonderful last night and I can't get over how lucky I was to see you dance the part.'

'To dance *Giselle* is something I've dreamed about ever since I started taking ballet lessons,' she replied. 'But I can't help wishing I hadn't achieved my ambition at someone else's expense.'

'What do you mean?'

'If Anya Merimée, the *prima ballerina* of the company, hadn't hurt her foot the night before last I'd have been dancing in the *corps de ballet*, as usual,' she sighed. 'I do hope Anya's foot will get better properly. The X-rays showed she'd broken two tiny bones. It would be dreadful if she couldn't dance again. She's such a great ballerina already and René predicts that one day she'll be as great as Margot Fonteyn.'

'And what does René Godin predict for Roselle Stanson?' enquired Adrian dryly as he lifted the champagne bottle from its bucket of ice and poured more wine into the two glasses. 'Surely he can't let you sink back into the anonymity of the *corps de ballet* after the performance you put on last night. You really had the audience involved in your suffering and misery during the Mad Scene.' He gave her a quizzical glance. 'I could almost believe you know at first hand what it's like for a girl to lose her reason because she's found out the man she loves has betrayed her and is going to marry another.'

He watched her closely for a reaction, but the wide greenish eyes never flickered away from his as, ignoring his comment, she answered his initial question.

'René says if I stay with his company he'll give me leading roles to dance now that I've proved myself,' she said coolly. 'But meanwhile I can honestly say I'm glad this season is over and I have a whole month in which to relax. Oh, you've no idea how much I'm looking forward to doing nothing, absolutely nothing!' She leaned back in her chair, flinging out her arms in an expressive uninhibited gesture as she laughed joyously at the thought of being free for four weeks.

'And where are you going to do nothing?' he asked. 'Here or in England?'

A faint frown clouded her fine-boned face as she picked up her knife and fork again.

'I'm not sure,' she muttered. She had nowhere to go really, had no relatives she could visit ... except one.

'Would you consider spending the time with me at a villa on the Riviera?' he asked.

Her reddish-brown hair which she was wearing that day in loose waves and curls spilling down to her shoulders glinted with fiery lights when she raised her head quickly again to give him another wide-eyed stare.

'Will anyone else be staying there?' she asked.

'I like that wariness of yours,' he murmured. 'It tells me you're a woman who puts a certain value on yourself, who isn't cheap or easy to get. My father, who owns the villa, lives there all the time now that he's retired from business. My mother will be with him.' He looked down at his glass. 'There will also be other members of my family,' he went on cautiously. 'Possibly one of my sisters with some of my nieces and nephews.' He looked at her again. 'I'd like my family to meet you,' he added softly. 'And that brings me to the real reason why I came to Paris this week and went to watch you last night. Roselle, I should like it very much if you would consider marrying me.'

For some time now she had been expecting him to make a proposition to her. After all, a wealthy middle-aged business man like Adrian Corwell did not pursue a practically penniless ballet dancer like herself across most of Europe for a whole winter and spring without having some sort of liaison in mind. But she had not expected him to propose marriage.

'You mean you would like us to be engaged?' she queried with pretended naïveté, playing for time, her thoughts darting in all directions as she wondered best how to tell him the truth about herself.

'That's the correct way of doing it, I believe,' he replied. 'Yes, I would like us to be engaged. I realise there are many differences between us. I'm more than twenty years older than you are.' A faint smile tugged at the corners of his thin-lipped mouth. 'Old enough to be your father, is the way it's put in all the best romances,' he added. 'Also I realise you have a career you wish to follow. Yet I feel we could manage very well together. I'm of independent means, so if you marry me I'll be able to support you and encourage you in a way that a younger man with ambitions of his own to satisfy could not.'

One of the waiters appeared, to take away their dishes. Another came to ask them what they would like for dessert. They consulted the menu with him, ordered, and he went away. Adrian poured more champagne and leaned across the table.

'Think, Roselle,' he went on persuasively. 'You would have no more worries about having to dance for your living. No more living in poky little apartments. No more trailing about all winter on tour with a small company. You would be able to pick and choose your roles. You'd be able to dance only those parts you feel most suited to dance. You could even start a ballet company of your own with my financial backing and of which you would be the star performer always. All you would have to do is be my wife.'

She looked away from him out to the shining blue-grey river, across the thick summer green foliage of trees to the pale stone of the soaring light-seeking Gothic arches of the ancient cathedral. She stared at it as if she was hoping for some answer to a prayer and with the tip of her tongue she moistened her lower lip. His offer was tempting because she was becoming tired of discomfort. If she married him life for her would immediately become luxurious in comparison to the way she had lived for the past few years. In fact marriage to him would solve many of the small problems of day-to-day living. And yet....

Slowly she looked at him. The bright sunlight was unkind to him. It showed up the flecks of silver in his smoothly brushed dark brown hair. Lines were scored heavily under his pale blue eyes and about his thin mouth. Old enough to be her father, he had said and, although he didn't know it, he was exactly the same age her father would have been if he had lived. Perhaps that was why she was attracted to him; he provided the father figure in her life she had never known. He represented security and protection. But to marry him?

'You hesitate,' he remarked. 'Have I surprised you?'

'A little.'

'And you won't consider my proposal?' he persisted.

'I ... er ...' She broke off and groped for her champagne glass. Lifting it, she drank the contents at one swallow. Maybe the sparkling wine would give her some courage to say what had to be said.

'Is there someone else?' he asked sharply. 'A younger man, perhaps, with whom you're in love?' He laughed rather harshly. 'Of course—why didn't I think of it before? An attractive young woman like yourself must have a lover....'

'Adrian, please,' she said quickly. 'There's something I have to tell you which might make you change your mind about asking me to marry you.'

'And what could possibly make me do that?' he argued teasingly. 'Come on, Roselle, tell me what awful skeleton you've been hiding in the cupboard.'

'I'm married already.'

He took her announcement well. His face paled only slightly and he blinked only once. But when he spoke his voice was hoarse.

'You ... you're....' He stopped speaking to clear his throat, then added with a touch of bewilderment, 'But why haven't you told me before?'

'I suppose I haven't because you haven't proposed to me before,' she replied as lightly as she could, remembering the other times she had been forced to tell an admirer she was already married and so not interested in marriage or in any other arrangement either. Odd how her marriage to Léon had acted as a defence all these years, a wall behind which she had been able to retreat.

The dessert came. It was a delicate soufflé flavoured with Grand Marnier. More wine was poured and the waiters went away. Roselle picked up her spoon and slid it into the creamy foam in the dish in front of her.

'You don't wear a wedding ring,' Adrian said suddenly and giving her an accusing glance. 'Why? Don't you have one?'

'Oh yes, I have one,' she replied, coolly returning his glare with a bland glance. 'I don't wear it for professional reasons.'

'And don't use your married name for the same

reasons, I suppose,' he muttered dryly, and she guessed from his tone he was hurt because she had allowed their friendship to reach this point without letting him know she was married. 'May I know what it is?' he asked politely.

'Chauvigny,' she replied in a low voice.

'So you married a Frenchman. When?'

'Five years ago, here in Paris.'

'Five years!' he exclaimed. 'Good God! You can't have been much more than....'

'I was just eighteen, old enough.'

'I can't agree,' he argued forcibly. 'At eighteen one is not old enough to make a serious decision like that. One is always changing one's mind, swinging to and fro from one enthusiasm to another, from one love to another, like a pendulum.'

'The decision was made for me. The marriage was arranged,' she said flatly, and again he looked astounded.

'By whom?' he demanded.

'By my godmother, Olga Valenska,' she replied, and laid down her spoon, suddenly unable to eat any more of the delicious orange-tangy soufflé. 'I think I've told you about her,' she added. He wasn't eating either but gazing at her from under frowning eyebrows, the expression in his eyes a mixture of puzzlement and exasperation.

'Yes, you have,' he said. 'She was a Russian ballerina who came to Paris before the second world war and danced for a while with the Paris Opera

Company and later with such famous companies as the Royal Ballet in London and the New York City Ballet. You said she opened a ballet school here in Paris when she retired from the stage and you trained at that school, but you didn't tell me she was your godmother. How did she come to be that?'

'Both my parents were ballet dancers, in England. They worked closely with Olga when she was in London and when I was born they asked her to be a godmother at my christening.' Roselle paused, sipped some champagne, then continued, 'They were both killed in an aircrash in South America when they were touring with a ballet company there. Olga took me under her wing and brought me to Paris to live with her and to teach me to dance as well.'

'How old were you then?'

'Nine.'

'Didn't you have any relatives in England who could have looked after you?'

'None who were interested in my future as much as Olga was. None who were as kind and loving as she was. You must understand, Adrian, that everything she did for me she did for nothing. My parents had no money to leave for my education.'

He finished his soufflé, emptied his wine-glass and wiped his mouth on his table napkin. Across the table he gave her a slightly pitying glance.

'And so naturally you felt under an obligation to her,' he suggested dryly.

'Yes, I did.'

'And when she asked you to do something for her you felt you had to do it. Am I right?' he queried shrewdly.

'It wasn't quite like that,' she retorted, trying to recall exactly how she had felt that day five years ago when Olga had come to her and had said Léon wanted to marry her. 'I wanted to do it not just to please her but also to ... to ... please myself.' She paused, gave him a quick wary glance and added in a whisper, 'But she was so worried about him, so desperately worried.'

'About whom?'

'About Léon. He was very ill, you see. He had some sort of fever which he'd picked up in Africa.'

'What had he been doing there?' he asked.

'I ... I think he'd been fighting in one of the wars that was going on at the time.'

'Fighting?' Adrian's eyes were wide with astonishment. 'Good God!' he exclaimed again. 'You mean to say he was a mercenary soldier?'

'Yes. You see, when he left school he went into the French Army to do his military service and when he'd done that he couldn't find any other sort of work which paid well. He was rather bitter about it and used to say he'd been trained only to fight and nothing else, so he signed on as a mercenary. But I wasn't really interested in what he did. To me he was just Léon who visited Olga whenever he was in Paris....' Her voice trailed off into silence as she was overwhelmed suddenly by memories of those visits by the handsome, mysteriously moody young man whom she had adored from the first time she had set eyes on him.

'So he wasn't a stranger to you,' said Adrian.

'No. I'd known him on and off for nine years. He's Olga's grandson, the only child of her only child, her daughter Anna. Like me he'd lost both his parents when he was a young boy. Olga was very fond of him and I suppose that was why she felt she had to help him when he needed help. When she asked me to marry him I had no hesitation in agreeing, and we were married in a bedroom at her house where he was lying ill.'

'Are you quite sure the ceremony was legal?'

'Quite sure. We signed a civil contract and also took vows before a priest.'

'And did Léon know what he was doing?'

Roselle looked away from his shrewd penetrating glance out at the river again. A faint breeze was rippling it now, silvering the blue with tiny cats-paws, but she hardly saw it because for a moment she was back in that bedroom in Olga's elegant Paris house looking down at Léon's unshaven face and tousled hair as he twisted his head restlessly in fever against the plump lace-edged silken pillows, hearing Olga Valenska's voice, sharply imperative, urging him to make the responses, and when he hadn't that same voice urging her to persuade him.

'Take his hand, Roselle,' Olga had murmured.

'Speak to him, tell him what to say.'

And she had taken the lean muscular hand in hers, had been shocked by its hot dryness and, kneeling down beside the bed, had whispered to him,

'Léon, oh, Léon, please open your eyes and look at me—please!'

The heavy lids had lifted and the dark fathomless eyes had looked right at her. A faint smile had slanted his mouth.

'Roselle,' he murmured. 'Little Roselle. When are you going to grow up?'

'I am grown up,' she had insisted. 'Léon, please tell the priest you want to marry me.'

'Do I want to marry you?' he had murmured.

'Yes. Your grandmother says you do.'

A frown had creased his forehead, his eyes had closed and he had muttered something unintelligible.

'Léon,' she had whispered again, aware of Olga prompting her. 'Oh, Léon, please say you will!'

His eyes had opened suddenly and he had looked directly at the priest.

'I will,' he had said firmly. The priest had nodded and the ceremony had continued with Léon repeating his responses after the priest clearly and intelligently.

Roselle sighed and looked across the table at Adrian.

'Yes, he knew what he was doing, I'm sure he did,' she said.

'It's amazing!' exclaimed Adrian, shaking his head. 'Quite Gothic. Or like one of those fairy-tale stories on which ballets or operas are based. So what happened next? Did Prince Léon, the mercenary soldier, get better and whisk you off to his castle somewhere, to live with him happily ever after?'

Roselle's eyes flashed with green fire as she took exception to his cynicism.

'If you're going to make fun I won't tell you any more,' she retorted. 'I've already told you more than I've ever told anyone else. I could have kept quiet, you know. I could have accepted your proposal and married you bigamously. Would you have liked that?'

Adrian looked startled at first by her reaction, then his expression changed to one of admiration.

'I'm sorry, my dear,' he said. 'You're quite right— I wouldn't have liked it if you had deceived me. What happened next?'

'Léon got better and went away,' she said flatly.

'Why? Where did he go?'

'I don't know why and I don't know where, or at least I didn't then. Later, a long time later, I found out he'd gone to Montenay.'

'But didn't you question that? I mean, having just been married to him didn't you think he would ask you to go with him?'

'Yes, I did, but you see Olga explained to me that

he had agreed I should carry on with my training as a dancer and one day when he had done what he had to do he would come back for me.'

'And you believed her, little romantic innocent that you were,' he taunted rather sadly.

'I had no reason not to. I wanted to finish my training,' she retorted, tilting her chin at him.

'And you were so used to doing everything Olga said you obeyed her without question, I suppose,' he remarked with a sigh. 'So you finished your training. What then?'

'I was auditioned by an English ballet company and they offered me a place in their *corps de ballet*. Olga encouraged me to take the position. I did and moved to London. I'd been living and dancing there for almost eighteen months when Olga died and I received a letter from her lawyer enclosing a letter she had written to me before she died. In it was Léon's address and so I wrote to him.'

'And?' Adrian prompted curiously.

'He came to London to see me,' she said quietly, faint pink colour staining her usually pale cheeks.

A waiter came to ask if they wanted coffee. They both ordered it and he went away. The restaurant was busy now, noisy with the voices of people as they lunched.

'Montenay,' murmured Adrian musingly. 'Where is that?'

'In Burgundy. It's a small estate enclosing a very well-known vineyard.'

'In the Côte d'Or?' he asked, his eyes lighting with interest.

'No. The department of Saône-et-Loire, near Tournus. It used to be owned by the Chauvigny family until Léon's paternal grandfather lost it when gambling. That happened when he was quite a young man and all his life he was trying to find ways to get it back. He used to take Léon there often when he was a boy and it was the old man's greatest hope that one day Léon would own it and there would be a Chauvigny as *le patron* at Montenay again. While the Arçenaut family owned it the vineyard deteriorated through neglect and mis-management. Then Paul Arçenaut, the son of Armand, died and the place was put up for sale. Léon heard about it and bought it.'

'Just after he'd married you,' Adrian guessed shrewdly. 'That was what he had to go and do, and once again there was a Chauvigny at Montenay. Where did he get the money?'

'He'd been saving all he'd earned as a mercenary, but he still didn't have enough, so he asked Olga for help.'

'She lent it to him?'

'She gave it to him. She gave him all the money she would have left to him in her will when she died,' Roselle replied woodenly.

'I see. Did you go with him to Montenay to live?'

'No.' She guessed he was probing, trying to find out what had happened when Léon had visited her in London. 'I wasn't prepared to give up my dancing career, so we decided to live apart,' she added coolly.

'Why didn't you get an annulment?'

'I don't know. We didn't discuss it.' Surely now he would take the hint and stop trying to find out just how close the relationship between her and Léon had been.

'Have you kept in touch with him during the past few years?' he persisted.

'We've corresponded a few times. Last September when I moved back to Paris I wrote and asked him if he wanted to do anything about our marital status.'

'Did he reply?'

'Eventually. He said he'd be quite willing to talk things over with me if I'd like to go to Montenay to see him some time soon.'

'How very magnanimous of him!' rasped Adrian sarcastically. 'You know the more I hear of him the less I like him. When did he write?'

'Six months ago. I didn't go to see him because I was too busy touring,' she replied defensively.

'Or you didn't want to go,' he put in dryly. 'You're afraid of him, aren't you?'

'I ... er ... perhaps I am,' Roselle admitted reluctantly, avoiding his intent stare. 'He isn't very easy to understand. Although I've known him since I was a girl he's still a stranger to me, a familiar stranger, if you know what I mean.' Again faint colour tinged her cheeks as she remembered just how familiar she and Léon had become when he had stayed with her in London.

'Mmm. I'm not surprised he's unpredictable,' murmured Adrian. 'He has an unusual heritage. Which part of Russia did Olga come from?'

'She was from Tartary.'

'Interesting. The Tartars were once a savage and intractable people, but they've produced some great dancers,' he mused. 'What about her husband? Was he Russian too?'

'Her first one was. She told me once he was a writer who had been imprisoned for his outspokenness when Stalin was in power. That was when she left Russia bringing her daughter with her to Paris. Later when she heard that her husband had died while he was in prison she married again, a wealthy Frenchman who left her very well provided for when he died.'

'And she gave it all to her beloved grandson to buy a vineyard,' remarked Adrian with a wry twist to his mouth. He tossed down his table napkin, rested his folded arms on the table and leaned towards her. 'Well, my dear, it's a most unusual story and I appreciate your honesty in telling it to me. But it hasn't made any difference to how I feel about you.'

'You mean....' She was a little startled. She had been quite sure he would withdraw his proposal.

'I mean I would still like to marry you. I'm very much in love with you and I'm not going to give up easily. I have to admit you had me worried for a few moments and I thought there were going to be difficulties, but now, as far as I can see, you'll have no problems in putting an end to this fairy-tale marriage of yours, especially since you and Chauvigny have never co-habited.'

'Oh, but I ... we ... I'll have to go and see Léon first,' she said quickly, playing for time again.

'I don't see why you should. It can all be done without you meeting him again.'

'But I can't just have a lawyer write to him,' she argued. 'There are things we ... Léon and I ... have to discuss privately.'

Adrian drained his coffee cup, glanced at his watch and signalled to one of the waiters. The man came, Adrian asked for his bill and the man went away.

'I have a meeting at three,' Adrian said briskly. 'And it's nearly two-thirty now. I'm sorry I can't spend the rest of the afternoon with you.'

'That's all right. I have shopping to do.' Roselle finished her coffee too. The waiter came with the bill on a small tray. Adrian produced a credit card and after studying the bill laid the card on the tray and the waiter went away again.

'Shopping?' Adrian queried, smiling at her.

'Yes. It's very necessary if I'm to go to Cap d'Antibes with you. I must have some suitable clothes—I haven't a thing fit to wear,' she said lightly.

'I can hardly believe that,' he said, his glance going admiringly over the silky long-sleeved shirt-waister dress she was wearing, the mixed blues and greens of which enhanced her fair skin. 'You're looking very charming today,' he added gallantly. Then he frowned and leaned forward urgently again. 'I'll drive you to Montenay on Friday,' he said autocratically.

'Why?' She was amazed and puzzled.

'So you can talk things over with Léon. I'd like to drive you down there before then, but I have to attend other meetings tomorrow. We'll go Friday morning and after you've seen him we can drive on by way of Lyons to the Riviera. I rather like that old north-south route to the Mediterranean, the way the Romans came into Gaul. And there are some interesting places along the way—Sens, Avalon, Cluny, Beaune, Mâcon. We could stop and browse through some of them, if you like. They're all crammed full of history and fine old buildings.'

'No!' Roselle spoke vehemently and loudly and the people at the next table stopped talking to turn and stare at her. But she couldn't help that. She had to stop Adrian somehow. He was moving too fast for her, trying to organise her life, hoping to stampede her into commitment to him.

'Why not?' he demanded.

'I would rather go and see him alone. I'll go by train to Dijon. It will take only two and a half hours and if I catch the *rapide* I can be there at nine o'clock—I expect I can get a bus to Montenay and back to Dijon in time to catch an evening train returning to Paris.' Seeing him frown, she reached out and touched him on the arm. 'Don't look so worried,' she teased him. 'I'm used to travelling about on my own—I've been doing it for years. I'll be quite safe.'

'I wonder,' he said.

'Oh, really, what could possibly happen to me on a train or a bus in the middle of a civilised country like this?'

'I wasn't thinking of what might happen to you on the way. It's when you get to Montenay I'm worried about,' he replied. 'I wish you'd wait until Friday and let me take you there.'

'I don't see what good your coming with me to see Léon would do,' she retorted stubbornly.

'I could give you moral support. I could even present your case for you. You know it's high time you made it clear to him that you can't go on like this tied to him in an old-fashioned sort of marriage arranged for you both by that old witch, his grandmother....'

'Olga wasn't a witch!' she flashed angrily.

'A fairy godmother, then. Much the same thing,' he sneered.

'She arranged our marriage for the best. She told me she did in her letter,' she said defensively.

'Fairy godmothers and people who arrange marriages always say that,' jeered Adrian. 'And she can't have been very good at psychology because it hasn't worked out, has it? You can hardly call it a perfect marriage.'

'I know that what she did must seem very strange to you, but I believe her intentions were of the best,' Roselle said in a low voice. 'The fact that it hasn't turned out the way she hoped is our fault—Léon's and mine.' She looked away, at the river again.

'My dear,' Adrian's voice was soft and concerned and his hand over hers was cool and gentle, 'I'm trying to understand. You've been trapped in this silly contrived situation and now you have a chance to do something about it. I've asked you to marry me and I'd like an answer soon, straight away in fact. I think that you'd like to accept my proposal but you can't say so until you're absolutely sure you can annul your marriage to Léon. So go and see him soon, please, not just for my sake or yours but also for his. For all you know he might want to be free too, to marry someone else, but he's just waiting for you to make the move.'

He was only saying what she had felt to be true for some time. And he was right; it was time she took some action.

'All right, I'll go and see him tomorrow,' she said.

'Very well, so that's settled.' He squeezed her hand comfortingly scribbled his signature on the credit flimsy the waiter had brought him. The waiter bowed, wished them both a pleasant day and pulled back Roselle's chair when she stood up.

'Shall we have dinner together this evening?' Adrian asked as he escorted her with a hand under her elbow to the lifts.

'I'd like to, but I promised Anya Merimée I'd go and see her. I'll phone you at your hotel tomorrow evening as soon as I come back from Montenay,' she said.

'To give me good news, I hope,' Adrian said softly as he followed her into a lift. 'And with that small crumb I'll have to be content until then, I suppose.'

Roselle was not very successful with her shopping. Talking to Adrian about her marriage had upset her more than she had revealed in the restaurant. It had aroused memories and had churned up emotions which she would rather have left sleeping. She found it impossible to concentrate on the serious business of choosing summer dresses and sports wear, suitable for wearing on the Riviera, and after a couple of hours wandering about various shops she gave up, hailed a taxi to the block of apartments where she shared a small one with another ballet dancer.

Her friend was out, so she had the place to herself. Feeling hot and sticky after her shopping expedition, she went through to her bedroom to take off her dress and shoes. She slipped on a long cotton housecoat and barefooted went to the kitchenette to make herself some tea. When she had poured herself some she carried the mug out to the small concrete balcony which fronted the long window of the living room. From there, perched half way up the eighteen-storey building, she had a view across roof-tops to the Eiffel Tower, a silhouette of dark inter-woven spider's webs of steel, reaching up against a sky which was already flushed gold by the upward-slanting rays of the afternoon sun.

Lying on a lounger, she sipped her tea and tried to relax, but inevitably her thoughts strayed to Léon. Tomorrow she was going to see him in reply to the letter he had sent to her six months ago, just as once he had gone to London to see her in a letter she had sent to him.

She tipped her head back against the padded cushion behind her and closed her eyes. How well she could remember that afternoon in late November when he had come to see her. It seemed to have been printed on her memory in indelible ink so that it could never be erased. Even now two and a half years later it was as if she were there, in London, returning to another apartment after spending an-other afternoon shopping.

CHAPTER TWO

THAT year, her second in London, she had rented a bed-sitting room in Putney, in one of the tall Edwardian houses which line the side streets just off the busy traffic-thronged High Street, a short distance from the River Thames. Once the houses had been private residences, but most of them were now converted and sublet as small apartments and bed-sitters, inhabited mostly by students, artists and other young people who earned a precarious living and had little money to spare for rent.

She always did her grocery shopping on a Saturday afternoon in the High Street and that afternoon the bitter wind of winter tweaked her headscarf and sliced through the woollen coat she was wearing over her jeans and sweater as she turned down the street where she lived. Shivering under the onslaught, she hurried along the wet leaf strewn pavement, walking with that strange stiff grace, her feet turned out, the typical walk of a ballet dancer who spent a lot of time on tiptoe.

Reaching the gate in front of one of the houses,

she opened it and went through, turned the knob of the front door and entered a long narrow hallway. Her arms full of grocery bags, she climbed the stairs, sniffing at the smell of steak and onions which was wafting up from a kitchen on the ground floor. On the second floor her attention was caught by the sound of voices raised in argument. It sounded very much as if Lucy and Glen Platt, the couple who lived together in the room beneath hers, were having another fight. Frowning, disturbed by their behaviour, she went up the last flight of stairs—and almost screamed with fright when a man stepped out of the shadows at the top.

He was of medium height, broad of shoulder. His face was lean and sun-tanned and he had very dark eyes—she had never been able to make out whether they were black or dark brown. In contrast with their darkness and the blackness of his eyebrows and lashes his hair was light amber. It fell across his forehead in a deep wave and curved thickly about his ears and neck.

'Léon!' she gasped.

'*Bonjour*, Roselle,' he said politely. 'I have come in reply to your letter.' He took an envelope from the pocket of the tan-coloured leather coat which he was wearing over a high necked black sweater and black pants. She recognised her hand writing on the envelope.

'I'm glad you've come,' she whispered, joy leaping up within her. She thrust the grocery bags at him. 'Please hold these while I look for my key.'

Once inside the fast darkening bed-sitting room they stood and stared at each other in silence. Léon spoke first.

'Where shall I put these?'

'Oh—over here, in the kitchenette.' She crossed the room to a curtained doorway and he followed her. Pulling back the curtain, she switched on a light and went into the tiny kitchenette.

'Put them there, on the draining board,' she said. 'When did you arrive?'

'I flew from Paris this afternoon,' he replied slowly in attractively accented English as he turned to face her. 'I arrived at this house fifteen minutes ago. The *concierge*. . . .'

'No, she's the landlady,' she interrupted him.

'Landlady, then,' he corrected himself. 'She said you would be back soon and that I could come up here and wait for you.' His glance went round the room 'You have only two rooms?' he asked.

'Yes. It . . . it's all I can afford right now,' she said quickly. 'But it's very comfortable and Mrs Tennant, the landlady, is a dear.' She was suddenly nervous because in the small room he was very close to her and was looking at her strangely as if he had never seen her before. 'Would you like a cup of tea?' she asked brightly, picking up the kettle. But she couldn't approach the sink to fill it because he was in the way.

'No, thank you. I don't like tea,' he said.

'Coffee, then?'

'*Non, merci.* Do you have any wine?'

'Only a little sherry,' she said, putting the kettle down on the stove again. 'It's in the sideboard in the other room.'

She went back into the sitting room and switched on the standard lamp. The rosy glow of light slanted down on the big chesterfield which would open out into a double bed, on the matching arm-chairs and coffee table, and added a sheen to the old mahogany sideboard which took up the whole of one wall and acted as a storage place for most of her belongings.

Taking off her coat, she slung it over a chair and went to the sideboard. She opened one of the side cupboards, groped for and found the half full bottle of sherry which had been there since the last time she had entertained a couple of friends to a meal. In the cupboard she found wine-glasses and took two out. Standing up, she put the bottle and glasses down on top of the sideboard and turned to Léon again.

'There it is. I hope it will do,' she said. 'I'm afraid I don't know much about wines, but I suppose we should have some to celebrate, shouldn't we?'

'Celebrate?' he queried, reaching past her and picking up the bottle to study the label on it.

'Yes. This is the first time we've met in two and a half years. I think it's cause for celebration, don't you?'

He put the bottle down and turned to scan her face with narrowed eyes. Again he pulled her letter out of his jacket pocket.

'Is it true, what you have written in this letter?' he asked coolly. 'Are we married?'

Air was cold and sharp against the back of her throat as she drew it in, gasping in surprise.

'Of course we are!' she exclaimed. 'Oh, don't tell me you've forgotten!' The memory of all that had happened in that darkened hot bedroom in Paris was so vivid to her she found it incredible he could forget such a momentous occasion. 'We were married in your grandmother's house on the Boulevard des Chevriers. I know you were ill at the time, but....' She broke off and going right up to him stared at his face with wide searching eyes. 'You said "I will" very clearly,' she whispered. 'And afterwards you put your grandmother's wedding ring on my finger.' She held up her hand so he could see the gleam of the wide old-fashioned ring and his dark glance shifted from her face to her hand and back to her face again.

'*Mon dieu!*' he muttered, and rubbed his forehead. 'It is true I have a vague recollection of some mumbo-jumbo like that.' His mouth took on a cynical curve and he gave her a penetrating stare. 'Are you sure it was a legal ceremony?' he demanded. 'You must forgive my doubts, *petite*, but Grand'-mère was always full of tricks and she liked to tease people. Often she would tease me and would make it difficult for me to get what I wanted by putting obstacles in my way which I had to overcome or by imposing conditions which I had to fulfil before she would let me have what I wanted.' He shrugged. 'But you must know what she was like about teaching self-discipline. It had become a fixation with her.'

'Yes, I know,' she murmured. 'But it wasn't a trick. It really happened, and I have a copy of the marriage contract which we both signed.'

'I signed something?' he exclaimed, a swift frown darkening his face.

'Yes. Your signature is a little shaky, but it is yours and I watched you write it. But haven't you got a copy of the contract?'

'No. Or if I had it has been mislaid somewhere.' His face hardened and his eyes glinted coldly at her, and in that moment it was easy for her to realise he had been a tough mercenary soldier paid to fight and kill. 'Show me the contract,' he rapped. 'Get it.'

Opening one of the drawers in the sideboard, Roselle drew out a big buff envelope in which she kept all important legal documents. She took out the marriage contract and turned to him. Before she could offer it to him he snatched it out of her hand and unfolded it. His mouth twisted bitterly at one corner as he read it through in silence. Then he folded it and handed it back to her. By the time she had replaced it in the drawer he had gone to stand at the window to stare down at the lamplit street.

Worried by his continuing silence, she went over to him.

'Do you believe we're legally married now?' she asked.

Léon swung round to face her and, alarmed by the controlled savagery of his movement, she stepped back a pace. Even in that shadowed part of the room she could see the murderous gleam in the depths of his dark eyes.

'Léon....' Instinctively she raised an arm before her as if to ward off an expected blow. 'What's the matter?'

He blinked, raised a hand, not to strike at her after all but to rake fingers through his hair, and his breath came out in a long ragged sigh. He half turned away from her.

'Nothing,' he muttered. Then he swung round again and to her relief the red glow had faded from his eyes and his mouth had softened. '*Oui*, I believe we are legally married now. That document looks very legal.' He laughed oddly and shook his head. 'I have been married to you for over two years and I didn't remember! All this time I have thought that what happened when I was ill at Grand'mère's house was the result of the fever, a fantasy produced by delirium.' He frowned again and gave her a puzzled glance. 'But why have you kept it to yourself all this time?' he demanded roughly. 'Why haven't you written to me before?'

'I didn't know where you were. You went away as soon as you recovered without saying anything to me and Olga told me you had agreed to let me finish my training as a dancer and that when you'd done what you had to do you would come back for me. I thought you must have gone back to fight in Africa and I always hoped I would get a letter from you. I didn't know where to write to you because Olga wouldn't give me your address. Not until I received a letter she had written to me before she died explaining why she had arranged the marriage between us did I know you were living in France.'

'The old. . . .' His straight white teeth snapped together viciously and he bit off something rude he had been going to say about Olga and gave Roselle another hard stare. 'You say she explained why she arranged the marriage,' he remarked. 'What reason did she give?'

'Just that she'd done it for the best because it was the only way she could think of to make amends to me for not leaving me any money in her will.' Roselle laughed a little. 'I'd never expected her to leave me any, so I didn't really understand what she meant. But I was glad to know where I could get in touch with you at last.'

'So you didn't know about the will she had made in which she intended to leave her money divided between the two of us?' he queried.

'No.' She stared at him in amazement. 'Was there such a will?'

'There was. And I knew about it. That was why I went to her and asked if I could have my share of the money before she died so I could buy back Montenay.'

'That's where you live,' she exclaimed. 'Is it a house?'

'It's more than a house. It's an estate in Burgundy with a well-known vineyard. It used to belong to my grandfather, Bernard Chauvigny, who inherited it from his father. He was foolish enough to use it as a wager when he was gambling once, and lost it to a man called Armand Arçenaut,' he said dryly. 'Grand'mère Valenska asked me how much I needed to purchase the place and said that instead of giving me just my share she would give me all the money on one condition.'

'And that was?'

'I would have to marry you and the money she would have left to you would be your dowry.'

It was as if he had put a pistol to her heart and had pressed the trigger. She swayed where she stood and caught hold of the nearest chair to lean on its back for support.

'I was taken aback, too, by her strange idea,' Léon went on as he noticed her shock. 'I hadn't realised she was so old-fashioned. But although I wanted the money badly I had reservations about agreeing to an arranged marriage to get it. I couldn't help thinking you were too young to be married to me and I didn't like the idea of Grand'mère thinking she could arrange our lives for us.'

'So what did you say to her?' Roselle whispered. Her throat felt choked and she couldn't look at him any more because tears of disillusionment had sprung to her eyes. Her youthful dream of romance was being smashed to pieces by his ruthless realism.

'I told her I'd think about it. I was thinking about it when I came down with that malaria relapse.'

'But she told me you wanted to marry me. I wouldn't have agreed to do it if I hadn't believed you wanted to do it too,' she said urgently.

'Then she tricked you,' he said, brutally honest, 'because I'm sure I hadn't agreed to her suggestion before I became ill. But it was on my mind and I thought afterwards that was why I'd imagined the ceremony had taken place.'

'Didn't she tell you we were married when you recovered?' she exclaimed.

'No.' He shrugged. 'I suppose she assumed I remembered the ceremony.'

'But when she gave you the money didn't you suspect that you might not have imagined it?'

'To tell the truth it didn't enter my mind. I supposed she had decided to relent and give me the money without imposing her crazy condition and I was keen to get down to Montenay and buy the place because I was afraid I might not get the chance again. You didn't seem to be around....' He paused and gave her a rueful glance. 'To tell the truth, *petite*, my mind was so full of Montenay that I didn't give you a thought. Not until your letter came this past summer. And I'm still finding it difficult to believe the Grand'mère actually went through with the marriage. She took advantage of both of us.'

'You're terribly angry about it,' she whispered. 'You're angry with me because I agreed to her suggestion, aren't you?'

His glance flicked to her face, lingered there, taking in the marks of dried tears under her eyes.

'No, not with you,' he said quietly. 'With her, for trapping someone as young as you were then into a marriage with someone like me. We had and we still have so little in common. I've led a rough and not particularly spotless life as a mercenary. Even now I live very roughly. My interests are in the land and what it can produce. I like growing things and working with animals. My world is very far from the delicate world of the ballet. Olga made a mistake when she married us.'

'But I don't feel trapped,' she argued. 'I've never felt trapped.' She went over to him. 'Ever since I first met you I've wanted to be married to you,' she confessed breathlessly.

His eyes widened incredulously before narrowing to dark assessing slits.

'What are you going to do now?' she asked nervously, not sure that she liked the calculating way in which he was looking at her.

'Make the most of the situation, of course,' he said softly. His glance went past her to the sideboard. 'Shall we drink the sherry now—that is if you still feel there is cause for celebration. Would you like me to pour it?'

'Yes, please.'

Roselle went over to the gas fire to light it because the room had grown cold. When she stood up he was coming towards her carrying the two glasses full to the brim. He handed one to her.

'We should drink a toast. To us and the future,' he said, and clinked his glass against hers.

'To us and the future,' she repeated, and felt hope begin to lighten her heart again.

'Come and sit down,' he urged, taking her hand and leading her to the settee. 'We still have a lot to talk about. Do you remember the hours we used to sit together in Grand'mère's *salon* whenever I visited her house in Paris?'

She nodded as she sat down beside him, feeling gladness spread through her in a warm glow because even if he had forgotten all about her when he had gone to live at Montenay at least he still remembered those times in Paris which were so precious to her.

'You were always so inquisitive,' he went on teasingly. 'Asking questions all the time. "Where have you been, Léon? What have you been doing? Where are you going now? When will you be back?"' He gave her a mocking sidelong glance. 'How old are you now, Roselle?'

'Almost twenty-one. My birthday is in April. And your birthday is ... oh, your birthday is soon. You'll be thirty on December the fifth.'

'What a memory!' he mocked. 'It's true.' The sardonic curve of his mouth mocked himself. 'I shall be over the hill this time next week.' He gave her another glance, much more serious this time. 'Do you want to stay married to me?' he said softly.

She sipped more sherry and studied the reflection of light in the wine before replying.

'Yes, I do,' she said at last, and gave him a swift, shy glance from beneath her lashes. 'But what about you? Do you want to stay married to me?'

He stared at the fire with half-closed eyes and drank the rest of his sherry. Then sitting up, he placed the empty glass down on the coffee table and turned to her.

'Since I don't know what being married to you or anyone else for that matter is like I can't answer that honestly,' he said with a touch of dryness. 'But I have heard it said that an arranged marriage is often more stable and successful than one which is based on romance because the partners don't expect too much of each other—and you have to admit ours was arranged very thoroughly by Grand'mère. So thoroughly that it would be difficult to untie the knot, at this stage.' His mouth curled with brief cynicism and there was a short silence as he glanced away at the fire again.

Roselle's heart was beginning to sink with disappointment again when he moved and leaned towards her.

'Is it agreed, then?' he said quietly in French. 'Shall we stay married to each other for the time being?'

The lack of romance in his approach was still disappointing, but she was glad he hadn't suggested an immediate annulment.

'It's agreed,' she whispered.

'*C'est bien,*' he murmured on a note of satisfaction, and leaned with indolent grace against the back of the couch. 'It is good to be here with you,' he said, 'and to have nothing to do for a while.' And he went on to talk of Montenay and how hard he had had to work during the past two and a half years supervising the replanting of the neglected vineyard.

'But this year the hard work paid off. This year's vintage was good and although the wine produced from it is not a great one it fetched a good price. But what about you? Have you been successful with your dancing?'

It seemed that everything was back to normal. Léon was once again the Léon she had known for so long, with whom she had often shared her hopes for the future.

'I'm still only in the *corps de ballet*, but I'm always hoping one day I'll get a chance to understudy a really great ballerina. Then perhaps my chance will come to dance some of the best leading roles. I'd like to dance *Giselle*, but Cynthia Faraday, the director of the ballet company I'm with now, says I'm too innocent, too lacking in emotional experience to be able to interpret such a tragic part.'

'That is what you would like to do most?' he asked.

'More than anything else in the world.'

'So it seems we are both ambitious. For you the ballet comes first and for me the restoration of Montenay comes first. That gives neither of us much time to spare for marriage,' he remarked. 'Do you have to dance tonight?'

'Oh, heavens, yes!' Roselle became suddenly aware of time passing and set down her empty sherry glass. 'I must go.' She turned to him urgently. 'You'll come and watch?' she asked. 'I can easily get you a seat in the theatre, and afterwards we could have supper together at a little restaurant I know, nearby.'

'I'll come. And after supper?'

'You could come back here,' she said shyly.

'Would you like me to?' he countered softly, sitting up again, close to her, his shoulder brushing hers, and for the first time since she'd known him she was physically aware of him, of the vibrant warmth which beat out from his body, of the smell of his skin and hair.

'Yes, please,' she whispered.

'Then I will.'

For a tense moment they sat poised looking at each other. Then with a swiftness which startled her Léon bent forward and brushed his lips tantalisingly against hers. At that warm sensual touch she stiffened slightly and pulled away.

'You shy away like a frightened bird,' he murmured. 'Why?'

'You ... you surprised me. I'm not accustomed to being kissed,' she replied.

'Am I to believe that you have never had a lover?' he said, ironic amusement curving his mouth.

'Of course I haven't,' she retorted. 'How ... how could I when I'm married to you?'

'So?' His eyebrows went up in mocking surprise. 'You have been faithful to me, hmmm? I'm afraid I can't say the same for myself, but then I didn't know I was married. It is no wonder that your Cynthia Faraday says you are lacking in emotional experience if you haven't had a lover.' He trailed a fingertip down her neck from the hollow behind her ear to the hollow at the base of her throat. 'I like that line,' he said, sliding his hand round to the nape of her neck. 'You aren't pretty, your mouth is too wide and your face is too thin, but one day you're going to be beautiful, *ma mie.*'

Strange sensations were shivering down Roselle's spine and she seemed to be mesmerised by his mouth; by the provocatively sensual curve of the lower lip and the severely beautiful chiselling of the long upper one. She wished his lips would come nearer and press against hers again. But they didn't. They just hovered closely and temptingly while he continued to stroke her neck.

Suddenly something seemed to explode within her. She could stand his teasing no longer. Reaching out, she framed his face in her hands, feeling the stubble of his hard beard rough against the softness of her palms.

'Oh, Léon, I do love you,' she whispered with youthful spontaneity, and rubbed her lips against his.

At once his arms swept about her, their hardness crushing her slenderness. Against his chest her breasts swelled and tautened. Ravaged by the bruising pressure of his lips, her lips parted willingly to the persistent thrust of his and all clear thought was swamped by the tide of desire which swept through her.

Slowly he withdrew his lips from hers. Facing each other, their breaths mingling, they leaned against the back of the couch gazing into each other's eyes, loving with looks.

'I must go,' she murmured reluctantly.

'Must you?' Léon leaned towards her and licked the corner of her slightly parted lips. 'You taste good and you feel good.' His hand slid down insinuatingly over her breast. 'Couldn't you miss the ballet for once? We have so much catching up to do, *ma mie*.'

There was sweet temptation in the soft suggestiveness of his voice and in the lingering intimacy of his caresses. She longed to give in and let the passion which was pulsing through both of them lead them on to ecstasy. But the self-discipline which had been drilled into her by Olga over the years asserted itself.

'I'd like to stay here with you,' she whispered, tracing the shape of his lips with a forefinger. 'But we're dancing *The Nutcracker* for the Christmas season and tonight is the first night. I dance a solo in it for the first time.'

'Then of course you must go,' he said immediately, and standing up he pulled her to her feet. 'We can talk later—all night if we want,' he added, drawing her to him and kissing her again, and as eroticism tingled deep within her and spread along her nerves like flames spread quickly and greedily through dry grass she knew that talking was not all they would do that night.

Later, knowing Léon was sitting in the blurred darkness beyond the footlights of the stage and watching her, she danced as she had never danced before and received not only loud applause from the audience but also praise from the director of the ballet. Yet it was a few words whispered by Léon as they sat later close together at a secluded candlelit table in a small restaurant near the theatre which brought her most joy.

'Grand'mère would have been proud of you. I am proud of you too, my lovely wife. *Grrr!*' he growled softly in her ear, 'I could eat and drink you. Mmm, *tu m'enivres*—you intoxicate me—and I think it is time you took me home to your bed.'

Light from the street lamps slanting through the window giving the illusion of moonlight streaked the unfolded bed where they lay and made love, and slowly with infinite tenderness Léon guided her along the paths of sensuous delight to a moment of passionate culmination when mind and body fused together in an explosion of joy.

Afterwards they slept for a while. When they wakened they talked lazily. He would stay, he said, for Christmas and the New Year. He could stay with her for a couple of months because there wasn't so much work to do on the estate during the winter.

'Would that please you?' he asked her, drawing her close to him, pressing her against his lean length, stroking her until every quivering nerve ending on her soft supple body was inflamed with desire.

'Yes, very much. You please me very much,' she said, and with a little moan of bitter-sweet anguish she hid her face against the pulsing warmth of his throat and murmured urgently, 'Please me again, Léon, please do it again!'

In the time afterwards, when he had gone back to France she could never hear the music of *The Nutcracker* without being overwhelmed by memories of those two months when he had lived with her in London. It was as if she had lived under a spell of magic, bewitched by the beauty and agony of loving him.

But the spell had broken one Monday morning in February on a day of soft sunshine and mild airs, deceptive, leading the unwary to believe that spring was on its way.

Roselle woke first and after lazily trying to wake him by ruffling his tousled amber-streaked hair which contrasted so dramatically with his olive-tinted skin and dark brows, she slid from the bed, pulled on her dressing gown and, gasping at the lateness of the hour, hurried into the kitchenette to put on the kettle for coffee. That done, she went down to the entrance hall to collect the newspaper and any mail.

There was only one letter. In a thick white envelope, it was addressed to Léon in sloping handwriting. The postmark and stamp were French and when she flipped it over she noted the name and address of the sender. It was from Angèle Arçenaut, Château Montenay.

Slipping the letter into the pocket of her gown, she returned to her room, made coffee, filled two mugs with the dark aromatic liquid, added cream and sugar and carried them into the living room.

Léon was still in bed, sleeping but stirring restlessly, twisting his head from side to side and muttering, and for a moment of dread she wondered if he was suffering from a malaria relapse. She set the coffee mugs down on a side table, sat on the side of the bed and laid a hand on his bare shoulder. To her relief his skin felt as usual, warm and supple, not dry and hot with fever,

'Léon, wake up! It's late, past eleven o'clock.'

'Stop it, go away,' he said quite clearly. 'Go away, Angèle.' Disconcerted by the strange name, Roselle leaned down close to him and kissed his cheek.

'Léon, please wake up,' she whispered.

She was unprepared for what happened next. His hand came up. He laid it flat against her face and pushed.

'Go away—for God's sake leave me alone!' he said. 'Can't you see I don't want you?' And heaving over on to his side he presented his back to her.

He had spoken so clearly and vehemently that it was easy for her to believe he was awake and was rejecting her advances to him, and for a few seconds she could only sit and stare, trying desperately to cope with the pain which sliced through her. Then her common sense asserted itself. Reaching out, she trailed a tormenting finger down the ridge of his spine.

'Leon, wake up, lazybones! I've brought you some coffee.'

He turned quickly, his eyes opened and he pushed himself up on his elbows to stare at her with sleep clouded eyes.

'I thought I told you to go away,' he began sharply, then broke off, his eyes clearing, and sagged back against the pillow with relief. 'I thought that

... I must have been dreaming.' He sat up again shaking his head from side to side. '*Mon dieu*, it was more like a nightmare,' he muttered.

'It sounded like it too,' she said, offering him the mug of coffee. 'You were grumbling and shouting all sorts of things. You had me quite worried, especially when you pushed me away and said you didn't want me.'

Over the rim of the coffee mug the dark eyes surveyed her warily.

'So I talked, hmm?' he murmured, and sipped more coffee.

'I thought at first you must have malaria again. Do you ever have a relapse these days?'

'I have had a couple since I went to live at Montenay, but neither were as bad as the one I had at Grand'mère's. I think it is cleared out of my system now.' He frowned at the coffee mug. 'I was dreaming about Montenay. It's time I went back there.'

Roselle remembered the letter and took it out of her pocket.

'This is for you. It's from Montenay, from an Angèle Arçenaut.'

'Good.' He set down the coffee mug and took the letter from her.

'You were talking to an Angèle in your sleep. The same one?' she asked lightly.

'*Oui*. I've been expecting a letter from her,' he said coolly and began to slit open the envelope.

'Who is she?'

'The housekeeper at Montenay.'

'Oh. I didn't know you had someone to keep house for you. You ... you never told me,' she complained, feeling a curious resentment building up inside her because Léon had never mentioned a woman before. 'Is the house so big?'

'*Pardon?*' he looked up from the letter. 'What did you say?' He tossed the letter to one side.

'I asked you if the house at Montenay is big?'

'*Mais oui.* It is a château, built in the sixteenth century. It has twenty rooms, far too big for a single man like myself to look after.'

'You aren't single,' she teased.

'*C'est vrai.*' His glance was warm. 'I wonder how long it will take me to remember that.'

'Arçenaut was the name of the man who won the place away from your grandfather when they were gambling, isn't it?'

'That's right. It's a common enough name, although Angèle claims to be a distant cousin of Paul Arçenaut, Armand's son, who inherited the estate when his father died. It was Paul who employed her as housekeeper.' His mouth twisted wryly. 'You could say she came to me with the house and the vineyard,' he added, yawning.

'Does she live in the house?'

'*Oui*, with her son Roger.'

'How old is he?'

'About two or three. I forget.' He yawned and shrugged.

'Then she's not an elderly woman.'

'Far from it. I suppose she's about your age. No, maybe a few years older, about twenty-four or five. I'm not sure.'

'Does her husband work on the estate?'

'She does not have a husband. Nor has she ever been married.'

'Oh.' Faint colour stained Roselle's cheeks as she digested this piece of information and realised Angèle's child was illegitimate. Léon watched the pinkness spread over her cheeks and his eyes danced with mockery.

'What time is it?' he asked.

'About eleven-thirty.'

'Then I must get going. If I am to be at Montenay by tonight I had better go to Heathrow immediately to catch a shuttle flight to Paris.' He swung off the bed and going over to the clothes he had taken off the night before, stripped off his pyjama pants and began to dress.

'Why do you have to go today?' she asked, eyeing the letter he had tossed aside suspiciously. 'Because your housekeeper has asked you to return?'

'I should have gone back last week,' he replied coolly. 'Now, I have to go today because some business concerning the estate has come up. I have to visit a notary tomorrow to sign some papers.' He went over to the door and stopped there, his hand on the knob to look back at her. A slight smile softened his face. 'I didn't go before because I didn't want to leave you,' he said softly, and went out, on his way to the bathroom which Roselle shared with the other tenants on the third floor.

Roselle watched the door close behind him, conscious of the frustration she had always felt when he had been evasive. She didn't want him to leave, yet she had known ever since he had arrived that this moment would come because the pattern had always been like that. Always he had come unexpectedly and unannounced and had left again, abruptly, without giving a reason for his departure.

She sighed. How little she knew about him! Oh, she knew so well, so intimately the shape of him, the colour of his hair and skin, the sound of his voice. She knew too, after the past two months, much about his tastes in food and drink. She knew what he liked to read and which music he preferred. But she knew no more about his innermost feelings than she had ever known. She knew nothing of his secrets.

She picked up the coffee mugs and took them through to the sink. How easily she had given in to him and had allowed him to stay, to move in and take possession of her, just because they had been legally married over two years ago. Yet she felt this morning that she possessed nothing of him. He was as elusive as ever.

What had happened between them would have happened anyway, whether they had been married or not, she argued with herself as she returned to the living room. Physical attraction between them was very strong and she had believed there was love between them too. She knew there was love on her part but suddenly she was no longer sure of his feelings for her.

She dressed quickly in slacks and a thin woollen sweater. Straightening the bedclothes, she began to fold up the bed-settee. The letter from Angèle Arçenaut fluttered to the floor. She picked it up and glanced at it guiltily.

'*Mon cher Léon.*' The words seemed to leap out at her. It was as she had begun to suspect; he and his housekeeper were on fairly intimate terms. She read on quickly.

'Monsieur LeFèvre, the notary, called to see you yesterday. He has been expecting you at his office and says the papers are ready for you to sign before February the fifteenth, so it is necessary that you return soon.

'I did not think you would be away in England so long. What has happened? Are you trying to get a divorce? How surprised I was when you told me you were married to a ballet dancer and intended to visit her. You do not behave like a married man!

'All is not well here. Roger has been sick and I have been run off my feet. It is time you came back to deal with your business affairs and with the men who work on the estate. Montenay needs a master. And so do I. Angèle.'

'I don't remember having given you permission to read any letters addressed only to me, *ma chère.*'

Although quiet, Léon's voice had an edge to it which warned her that he was angry as he came back into the room. Folding the letter, Roselle turned to face him. Freshly shaved, his hair damp and smooth, his skin smelling rather exotically of her Yardley's rose-perfumed soap, he came right up to her and took the letter from her.

But she was too angry herself, too racked by an all-consuming jealousy, born of her unsureness where he was concerned, to apologise or back down in any way. Tossing her hair behind her shoulders, she returned his angry glare with one of her own.

'She writes to you very affectionately for a house-keeper,' she accused.

'Angèle is like that. She overflows with affection.' Léon gave a short laugh. 'No man is safe from her attentions.'

He shrugged dismissingly, pushed the letter into his pants pocket and went over to the clothes closet where the few clothes he had brought with him to London were stored with hers. Taking out a shirt, he began to pull it on.

Roselle watched him, suspicions growing fast in her mind.

'Is she your mistress?' she asked, voicing the thought which was uppermost. He didn't reply and taking his zipped leather valise out of the closet he began to push clothes in it.

'I remember you saying the day you came here that you hadn't been faithful to me during the two and a half years we've been married,' she went on, driven by the devilish jealousy, unable to leave well alone. 'I suppose she's one of the women.'

He gave her a sharp underbrowed glance but still said nothing and continued to pack the bag. Bewildered by the storm of hate which the letter from Angèle had stirred up in her and which was blinding her to the danger signals, Roselle wished he would stop what he was doing, come over to her and take her in his arms to kiss away her doubts and suspicions.

'Léon, please say something,' she whispered desperately.

He zipped up the valise and sat down on the nearest chair to put on his shoes.

'What would you like me to say?' he said coldly. 'Would you like me to lie to you and say there have been no women in my life except you?' His glance was chillingly derisive as it raked her. 'I've not spent the adult years of my life in a monastery, you know,' he added sardonically. 'I've been a soldier, not a monk.' He laced up his shoes quickly and standing up, came towards her, at last, a smile beginning to curve his mouth. 'Listen, *petite*. My relationship with Angèle or with any other woman is no concern of yours and. . . .'

'Yes, it is,' she insisted. 'I'm your wife.'

'That does not mean you own me.' It came out sharply, a flicking knife to warn her she was assuming too much. 'Nor does it give you the right to read my letters or probe into my past affairs.'

They stood facing each other and Roselle felt desolation creeping into her heart because after all the lovely time they had had together she was no closer to him. She might bear his name, sleep with him and make love with him, but he wasn't hers.

'Then what rights does it give me?' she asked, and he gave her another exasperated glance.

'I might have known you would behave like this,' he said, his eyes glinting dangerously. 'You always were possessive. Do I have to remind you of the terms of our marriage? It was arranged for us and so we should not expect too much of each other.' His breath hissed raspingly as he drew it in. 'For example, I'm not expecting nor insisting that you come with me to Montenay today just because you are my wife. I know that for you the ballet must come first and you'll want to stay here and dance until the season is over.'

'I don't believe that's why you don't expect me to go with you,' she stormed. 'You don't want me to go because you want to be alone with this ... this Angèle. You're going back because she asked you to go and you would rather be with her than with me!'

'That isn't so,' he retorted quietly, turning away to pull on his black sweater. 'I'd like you to come later in the year, when the ballet season is over. You could come in the summer. It is beautiful then, when the grapes are ripening on the vine. You might stay for the vintage.' His mouth quirked with wry humour. 'After all, the place is partly yours, bought with the money given to me as your dowry, so you should come to see it and live there for a while.'

Now he was humouring her as he had always humoured her when she had been a girl, putting her off with promised sweets, as an elder brother might humour a younger sister. But she was past being treated like his sister and her pride came rushing up.

'I'm not sure I'll be able to come then,' she said stiffly.

'Why not?' He was only casually interested, it seemed, as he put on his leather coat.

'There's talk of the company going on tour to Australia and New Zealand this summer and I'd like to go. It will be good experience.'

'You see?' he said equably. 'It is as I had thought. You have your life to live and I have mine.' He pushed back the wave of hair from his forehead. His eyes, pitch-dark above the high Tartar cheekbones he had inherited from Olga, studied her closely. 'You would be wise to take the opportunity to go on tour. It will benefit your career, I can see that. You can always come to Montenay another time,' he added.

But when shall I see you again? The words sang through her mind like a refrain from some bitter-sweet 'pop' ballad, but she didn't utter them. Pride prevented her. Taking her cue from the indifference expressed in his face, guessing that mentally he had left her already and was on his way across the Channel to France, she turned away from him.

'Why did you come here?' she muttered in a dull lifeless voice. 'Oh, why did you come?'

'I came to see you and to find out if our marriage was legal. It was. And still is.'

'So you made the most of it,' she accused miserably, swinging round to face him again. 'You moved in, took possession, took advantage of me.'

'Did I?' Léon shrugged carelessly. 'Perhaps. But I doubt very much if any man with blood in his veins would have behaved differently on finding himself married to a woman as enticing as you are and who offered what you offered so freely to me.' His glance swept over her insolently. 'Nothing was done without your agreement,' he said flatly.

'I did not offer to. . . .' she began furiously, saw the black eyebrows go up in derision and the dark eyes glint with irony and burst out, 'Oh, go away, get out . . . you . . . you mercenary! Go back to Montenay and your housekeeper and see if I care!'

Threatened with tears, she whirled away from him and rushed into the kitchenette where she began to open and close cupboard doors noisily in her search for the frying pan. She would have bacon and egg for breakfast, she thought wildly, because he disliked it.

'Roselle,' Léon spoke quietly from the curtained doorway.

'Oh, go away, go away!' she cried. 'And don't come back.'

'Don't worry, I'm going,' he retorted. '*Au revoir, petite*. You might write and let me know if you're going on that tour.'

For several weeks after he had left Roselle was very unhappy, missing him dreadfully, and she spent many sleepless nights going over everything which had happened between them, often wishing she had never read that letter Angèle Arçenaut had sent. If she hadn't seen it she wouldn't have quarrelled with Léon, wouldn't have said what she had said to him.

The weeks went by. She heard nothing from him and gradually she became convinced that she had been right after all and he had used her worshipping adolescent love for him to his own advantage and self-gratification while all the time he reserved his love for another woman, possibly the housekeeper. If he had loved her, she argued, he would have insisted she go with him to Montenay. If he had loved her he wouldn't have been able to leave her. But he didn't love her, and he had betrayed her love for him.

Spring came. The ballet season drew to a close. Roselle was chosen to go on tour with the company and she decided to go. Although her sensitive spirit was still smarting from the experience of those two months with Léon, she had come to terms with her unhappiness and was able to write and tell him she would be going with the company to Australia and New Zealand.

Perhaps she had hoped he would come to London then, play the domineering husband and demand that she go with him to Burgundy to live with him because he had discovered he couldn't live without her, because she had been very disappointed when he had written instead, a pleasant letter thanking her for informing him of her plans and suggesting again that she go to Montenay another time.

As for himself, he was too busy to visit her in London again that year. Maybe the following year he would come if she was still with the ballet company there. It would all depend on the vintage.

Roselle sighed and shivered, coming back to the present. Beyond the elegant Eiffel Tower the sky was now flushed with crimson. Lights were twinkling all over the city. Night had come to Paris, the time when the city was at its most exciting and romantic. She swung off the lounger and lingered for a moment watching the traffic streak by far below in a constant glittering stream of white and red light.

Léon hadn't visited her again in London, nor had he come to see her in Paris when she had written to him last September. And she had never gone to Montenay. But she felt that time had done its usual work of healing and now it was safe for her to see him again. His betrayal of her love for him had not made her go mad as Albrecht's betrayal of Giselle in the ballet had caused that innocent loving girl to go mad. But it had forced her to grow up, as it had cured her of her love for him. So there was no possibility of him taking advantage of her again. No chance at all of him making the most of the situation.

CHAPTER THREE

THE next day started badly. Roselle, having stayed late at Anya Merimée's the previous evening, overslept and as a result did not catch the early morning *rapide* to Dijon. Although she knew that going by a later train meant that she would not have as much time at Montenay as she had expected she went on it anyway, but it took longer than the usual two and a half hours, slowed down because part of the railway track was being re-laid on that route. As a result she didn't reach Dijon until noon, by which time she had missed the bus going to Bezalay, the town nearest to Montenay, and she had to wait half an hour for the next one.

It was then she should have given up and returned to Paris, she thought fretfully, as she sat beside a window on the bus looking out at sun-bathed hillsides, green-gold vineyards and lush green valleys of the Burgundian countryside, for the bus was taking the long way round to Bezalay, stopping at every farm to let off passengers or take them on, and by the time she reached Montenay it would be past two at this rate of progress and time for her to go back.

She wished she had planned her trip more carefully, and tried to get in touch with Léon, arranged to meet him in Dijon. They could have discussed their problem quite satisfactorily over lunch in one of the excellent restaurants there. Or she could have taken Adrian's advice and not come at all but let a lawyer handle the whole business.

The bus trundled into yet another town of limestone houses. But here there was a difference. Instead of being steeply pitched the roofs of red tiles were almost flat, indicating that the climate was different from the area around Dijon and that there was no fear of snow. The bus swung up a narrow twisting cobblestoned street past a simple yet splendid Romanesque church and came to a stop in an open sunlit square in front of the Hotel de Ville.

'*Ici* Bezalay,' droned the driver, and Roselle got up from her seat and went down the aisle to speak to him.

'Could you tell me how to get to Montenay from here?' she asked.

'Do you wish to go to the village of Montenay or the Château of Montenay?' he growled.

'The Château.'

'Then stay on the bus. Montenay is between here and Mâcon.'

'How long will it take to get there?'

'About twenty minutes, give or take a few. It isn't

far. I'll tell you when we're there.'

His twenty minutes was an optimistic estimation because twenty minutes later the bus was still meandering about the countryside as if the driver had lost his way and Roselle was beginning to think that Montenay did not exist. But at last they reached another smaller village, a single street of flat-topped houses surrounded by roses and rows of vines which covered hundreds and hundreds of acres as far as the eye could see. An old man who was getting off the bus nudged Roselle as he passed her, his blue-grey eyes twinkling cheerfully in his lined red-cheeked face.

'Not far now, *mademoiselle*,' he croaked. 'The Château is only four kilometres from the village. You can't miss it. It sits on a hill and its walls glow like a good Beaujolais wine.'

'*Merci, monsieur.*'

The bus started up again. There were many more passengers on it now, mostly women on their way to Mâcon. Past more rows of vines it twisted and suddenly in the distance Roselle caught the glow of pink against a hot blue sky. Slowly as the bus followed the winding road the glow developed shape, became a cluster of buildings on top of a hill surrounded by a creeper-covered wall.

'*Ici* Château Montenay,' called the driver as he brought the bus to a stop at the end of a lane which arrowed between stately poplar trees straight up to the buildings on the hills. 'You will have to walk from here,' he said to Roselle, giving her a critical glance. *'Bonne chance!'*

She waited until the bus had gone before turning into the lane. How far was the château? About a kilometre, she reckoned, and she set off at a quick pace.

It was very hot, the breathless heat of a summer afternoon in the middle of France and she was glad of the shade cast by the poplars. The heavy air was scented by vines and other plants and there was no sound, not the rustle of a leaf nor the twitter of a bird.

The narrow road was rough and stony, hard on the feet, especially when you were wearing high-heeled thin-soled sandals as she was. Several times she had to stop to slide a finger between the sole of her foot and a sandal to remove small stones which had lodged there and were pricking her.

The heat and the silence made everything seem a little unreal. It was like walking in a landscape painting. Was she really there on her way to the château? Was that house on the hill, gleaming like some fantastic jewel in its lush tranquil setting of sloping green meadows dotted with white Charollais cattle, really the place where Léon lived? Or was it a mirage only, produced by the heat and beckoning her on? She didn't seem to be getting any nearer to it. Perhaps she would never reach it. Perhaps she would wander for ever, never getting any nearer to it or to Léon.

She glanced at her watch and frowned. It was almost three o'clock. She must hurry. If only it wasn't so hot! Her dress was clinging to her. She felt like taking it off, her sandals too, and running into the long grass starred with buttercups and other wild flowers which stretched beyond the poplars towards the blue-grey sheen of a small river which wound snake-like along the floor of the valley.

The heel of her left sandal turned on a stone and her ankle twisted over. Pain stabbed through that sensitive place and she gasped. She would have to be careful about where she stepped, slow down a little. It wouldn't do for her to sprain her ankle or break a bone in her foot as Anya had done. *Ouch!* The heel turned again and the same agonising pain speared upwards. Gingerly she stepped forward again. The ankle, weakened by the two twists, gave way, she lost her balance and fell to her knees.

Feeling hotter than ever, sweat breaking out on her forehead and under her arms, she scrambled up, dusted her dress down, biting her lip to hold back a desire to burst into tears because of the pain, then cautiously set off again, only to realise that she had lost the heel off her left shoe altogether.

Oh, it was too much! The day had been nothing but a disaster. Wincing with pain from her ankle, she limped to the side of the road and sat down on the stump of a tree which had been cut down. Overgrown with lichen and fungus, it was badly decayed, but it was still possible to sit on it and Roselle sank

down thankfully. She slipped off her now useless
left sandal and examined her ankle. A dark and
ominous swelling was forming between the ankle
bone and the instep.

She should never have come. She should have
gone back from Dijon. Seeing Montenay, meeting
Léon again, wasn't worth damaging her foot and
possibly ruining her career as a dancer. And what
was she going to do? There was no one about. The
meadows and rows of vines were deserted. She would
have to sit here until her foot seemed a little easier
and then limp on to the house.

'Man proposes, God disposes.' The old adage
came into her mind to torment her as she sat there
hearing bees and other insects buzzing amongst the
grasses. She had intended to arrive at Montenay
looking cool and poised, dressed as only someone
from Paris could dress, to prove to Léon she was no
longer the adolescent girl he had married and no
longer the naïve young woman he had seduced when
he had visited London. But now it looked as if she
was going to arrive looking a mess, her dress ripped
where she had fallen on her knees and her hair falling down from the chignon into which she had
coiled it.

Well, at least she could do something about her
hair while she sat there. She opened her handbag
and took out a mirror and was busy with a comb
when her ears picked up a sound which was louder
and more powerful than the persistent buzz of the

wasps which were hovering about the tree-stump. A vehicle of some sort was going along the main road. Too much to hope it was coming her way, she supposed—and then felt her nerves quiver in anticipation as the sound altered, faded, then started up again when the engine changed gear. Definitely it was coming this way.

Pushing mirror and comb into her handbag, she slung it over her shoulder and picking up her discarded sandal hopped into the middle of the lane. She could see the vehicle now. It was a farm truck, the sort used to convey vegetables and fruit to market. It was coming quite fast and after waving her white handbag at it Roselle stepped quickly to the side of the road in case it couldn't stop before it reached her. There were two people sitting in its cab, she noticed. Was it possible one of them was Léon?

The lorry pulled up sharply, churning up a cloud of dust from the rough surface of the road, and above the noise of its clattering engine a female voice called out from the window nearest to Roselle.

'*Qu'est-ce qui arrive?* What has happened?'

Roselle hopped up to the lorry. A woman of about twenty-five, big and broad, with golden-brown hair, dark brown eyes and cheeks which glowed like peaches, looked down at her curiously.

'I have sprained my ankle, I think, and can't walk very well. Could you give me a lift to the Château, please?' Roselle asked.

The woman's face expressed sincere concern. Turning, she said something to the man who was sitting beside her and who wasn't Léon, then she opened the door and stepped down from the lorry.

'Ah, what a pity!' she exclaimed, her glance going to the foot which Roselle was holding poised above the ground. 'Quickly, Pierre, come quickly, and lift *mademoiselle* into the cab.'

'No, it's all right—I can get up myself,' Roselle began.

'I do not think so, *mademoiselle*,' said Pierre. He was also big and muscular and not unlike the woman, although his hair was darker. He was wearing the rough denims of a farm worker and under his thick drooping moustache his teeth glinted in a smile as he approached Roselle. He lifted her easily as if she were a doll and within a few seconds she was sitting in the long front seat of the lorry. The woman climbed up beside her. Pierre took his place behind the steering wheel and with a grinding of gears the lorry moved forward.

'So it is to the Château you wish to go,' said the woman. 'Whom do you wish to see there?'

Her curious brown gaze was flicking over Roselle's silky full-skirted dress.

'I'm going to see Monsieur Chauvigny—Léon Chauvigny,' replied Roselle. 'He lives at the Château ... at least ... I mean ... he does still own Montenay, doesn't he?' she added a little nervously. For all she knew Léon could have sold the place or gone back to soldiering.

'*Mais oui*, he still owns Montenay and he is at home today. Is he expecting you? He mentioned nothing to me about expecting a visitor today.' The woman smiled genially in response to Roselle's surprised glance of enquiry. 'I had better introduce myself. I am Angèle Arçenaut, housekeeper at the château, and this is my brother Pierre who works also for Monsieur Chauvigny.'

Roselle felt a little strange. So this big sensual woman was Angèle from whose attentions no man was safe! Yes, she could see the motherliness, the overwhelming affection Léon had once mentioned in the placid almost cow-like eyes, the plump cheeks and the big burgeoning bosom over which a simple sleeveless cotton blouse could only just stay fastened.

'I'm Roselle Stanson,' she introduced herself, half turning to nod at Pierre.

'Is that so?' Angèle's loud voice shrilled with amazement and Roselle turned back quickly to her. The big brown eyes were rounder and wider than ever. 'Then you are the wife of *le patron*?'

'Yes ... but how did you know? Stanson is my stage name. I didn't think you would recognise it and. ...'

'But of course I know,' Angèle cut in, smiling again. '*le Monsieur patron* has told me about you. You dance in the ballet, *n'est-ce pas*? And you used to live with his grandmother in Paris.' Angèle leaned forward to speak to her brother. 'Pierre, this is Madame Chauvigny come home at last,' she said.

'Welcome home to Montenay, *madame*.' Pierre's smile was also genial.

'Thank you,' said Roselle faintly. She was feeling slightly embarrassed by their warm welcome. What would they say when they found out she had come for only a few hours? What would they say when they learned she had no intention of remaining as Madame Chauvigny?

The lorry chugged up a steep incline, swept under an archway in the thick creeper-covered wall and came to a stop in a sunny courtyard ablaze with the exotic colours of all sorts of flowers; yellow and crimson begonias, golden double marigolds, scarlet and pink geraniums, the blue spikes of delphiniums and even the white and rose-pink bells of foxgloves.

Near at hand the limestone of the Château's walls glowed ruby red and as Pierre carried her into the house and along a cool stone-floored passage Roselle felt again as if she were experiencing a fantastic dream from which she would soon wake up and find herself in Paris.

The room into which she was taken was furnished as a small *salon* with graceful couches and shining side tables and cabinets. Blue-grey damask curtains framed two long French windows which opened on to a terrace and the same colours and patterns were repeated in the wallpaper. Thick rough wooden beams criss-crossed the low ceiling, an indication of the age of the house.

Pierre set her down on one of the couches, she thanked him and he departed. Before she could say or do anything else Angèle was squatting before her and examining her ankle.

'Ah, it is swelling nicely,' said the housekeeper. 'That is good. But it should be bathed. I'll go and fetch some hot water.'

'Please would you. . . .' Roselle began, and stopped because the housekeeper, ignoring her, had already left the room.

Perhaps she intended to tell Léon he had a visitor while she was getting the water, thought Roselle, leaning back with a sigh and raising her injured foot to a small tapestry-covered footstool.

The room was cool and quiet, scented by the huge bowls of flowers which had been arranged in the stone fireplace and on the big carved buffet which stood against one wall. But now that she was able to look more closely she could see that although neat and clean, it was very shabby. The upholstery was threadbare and the blue-grey carpet was worn in many places.

'This will ease the pain and draw the swelling out more,' said Angèle practically as she returned to the room with a big aluminium bowl full of steaming water which she set in front of Roselle.

'Have you told Léon ... my husband ... I'm here?' Roselle asked tentatively as she slid her left foot into the water. The heat was soothing to the dry dusty foot.

'Pierre has gone to find him. He is working among the vines on the other side of the valley today,' said Angèle. 'Have you come far today, *madame*?'

'From Paris.' Roselle spoke warily, remembering the suspicions she had once had about this woman.

'So you have had a long journey. You must be thirsty and perhaps hungry too. Would you like some lemonade? Or would you prefer tea?'

'Lemonade, please,' replied Roselle gratefully, and watched the woman go from the room, wishing contrarily that she did not have to depend on her.

Le patron, Angèle had called Léon. The master, and there had been a note of respect in her voice. Difficult to imagine that she had once addressed him as *mon cher* in a letter. But then it was difficult too to imagine the young mercenary soldier she herself had known since she was a girl as master of this beautiful old house and of all that land out there. Now having seen Montenay she could understand his obsession with it. Generations of his French forebears had lived here and had made wine here. It was in his blood and so it was only natural that he should want to be here.

Angèle padded back into the room carrying a tray on which there was a tall glass of lemonade and a plate of biscuits. She set it down on a small side table which she drew close to Roselle and then sat down on the footstool. She draped a towel which she had brought across her knee.

'And now let me look at your ankle again,' she said. 'Ah, I think it has swelled enough. I'll dry it—and I think it best, *madame*, if you rest it for a while, stay on this couch with it supported on a cushion, like so.' She arranged a velvet-covered cushion under the ankle. 'Later, if you like, I'll bandage it, to give it support. But it will be best if you don't walk on it at all. . . .'

'But I'll have to,' Roselle interrupted her. 'I have to go back to Paris tonight. Isn't there anywhere near here where I could borrow some crutches?'

'Crutches?'

'Yes. Sometimes it is possible to hire them from a pharmacy. . . .'

'But there is no pharmacy here, *madame*. The nearest one is in Tournus.' Angèle was picking up the bowl of water. 'I'll bring you something to read while you are waiting for *le patron*. It will help pass the time for you.' And with another benign smile she left the room again.

The housekeeper was very kind—too kind, overwhelmingly kind, and it would be difficult to stop such a person from overwhelming you with her affection, thought Roselle. And if you were a man and she lived in the same house as you. . . . She had to snatch her thoughts back from the direction in which they were wandering. It didn't matter to her how kind Angèle was or had been to Léon. It didn't matter if the woman was or had been his mistress.

It didn't matter to her because she was no longer in love with him.

She groaned and buried her face in her hands. It had been a mistake to come. She should have left well alone. If she could walk now without pain and without fear of making the injury to her ankle worse she would be out of here in the next few minutes, going down the lane in the hope of catching the bus on its return journey to Dijon. She would leave before Léon came in, before she saw him again.

She swung her legs off the couch and cautiously tried to stand up, putting her weight on both feet. Pain twinged through her ankle. It was no use; she couldn't walk. She was stuck here and had to wait until Léon came. But once he came she would ask him to drive her straight back to Dijon.

Angèle brought her some rather old, tattered magazines and left the room again. Roselle leafed through them, aware of time passing by, of sunlight shafting into the room through the windows as the sun moved inexorably round to the west and the clock on the sideboard chimed the hour and then the half hour. Four o'clock, four-thirty, five o'clock, and still no sign of Léon. No Angèle either, for the housekeeper had not returned to the room to check on her patient.

Restlessly Roselle swung her legs off the couch again. This time she did not try standing on her injured foot but holding it clear of the floor she hopped on her right foot to one of the windows.

Beyond the edge of the terrace she could see the green-gold land sloping down to the shining river. On the other side of the river half way up the slopes the straight rows of vine slanted up and beyond them were the thick woods topping a range of hills, dusky blue now against the sun-bright western sky.

Where was Léon? Working on the other side of the valley Angèle had said, over there among the straight rows of vines. Why didn't he come? Why didn't he stop what he was doing and come running, knowing she was here? Roselle's mouth twisted in a rueful smile. Why should he come running just because she was there? Why did she expect so much of him?

Impatient with herself, she hopped back to the couch, pausing beside it to hold on to the carved back, and in that moment she heard voices and footsteps in the passage. Angèle's voice, strangely high-pitched for such a big woman, and a lower, deeper masculine voice speaking roughly, dictatorially. Léon's?

Roselle felt herself quiver with excitement. In the next moment she was admonishing herself for reacting in such a way to the sound of his voice. Still standing, she supported herself with one hand on the back of the couch. Better to be on her feet when he came in. Better to greet him that way, to face him coolly.

Léon swung through the archway which was the entrance to the room from the passageway and came

to a dead stop when he saw her. She saw his eyes
widen slightly, but that was the only sign he gave
of being surprised to see her. Then he half-turned
away to look down the passage as if in search of
Angèle. Turning towards her again, he came across
the room in a few graceful strides.

'Roselle,' he said. 'Ah, *ma mie*, it is good to see
you!' And before she could move he had stepped
round the couch up to her. His arms went about her
and she was swept against him. She had a brief
glimpse of Angèle hovering in the archway watching and then her face was tilted up forcibly by a
rough tanned hand which smelt of soil and vines
and her mouth was crushed by his in a bruising kiss
which punished rather than welcomed her. Under
that onslaught her mind reeled dizzily and involuntarily her hands went out to clutch at the rough
denim of his shirt.

He raised his head. She opened her eyes, saw in a
blur the amber-streaked hair tumbling over his forehead, the slightly slanted eyes glinting wickedly at
her.

'I had forgotten how good you taste,' he murmured, and bent his head to kiss her again, but on
the alert now, furious with herself for having suc-
cumbed for even one brief moment, she turned her
head quickly and the kiss landed somewhere on her
hair. Over his shoulder she noticed Angèle had
gone, so she put her hands on his arms and pushed
him away.

'That was quite a performance,' she jibed coolly. 'But you can stop now. Angèle has gone.'

His eyes narrowed unpleasantly and he let her go so suddenly she lost balance and had to put her left foot to the floor. Pain sliced knife-like through her ankle and she yelped.

'What's the matter?' he demanded, frowning at her.

'My ankle. I think I've sprained it—I can't walk on it,' she muttered.

'Then you had better sit down, hadn't you,' he said with familiar dry practicality, and again before she could move lifted her into his arms as Pierre had done earlier. But when Pierre had held her she hadn't gone hot all over like this, nor had her heart raced.

When she was lying on the couch again he sat on the edge close to her and took hold of her left foot in his hand. Against her cool skin his hand seemed to burn. The fingers stroked gently yet tantalisingly over the swelling and trailed almost suggestively up the shin of her leg. Shifting position, she twitched her leg away from that possessive, insinuating touch of his and crossed it over her other leg.

'It does not look so good,' he said. 'How did you sprain it?'

'Walking up the lane here. Didn't your house-keeper tell you how she and her brother found me and gave me a lift?'

'They told me only that I had an unexpected visitor.'

'It took you long enough to come,' she said rather acidly.

'It took Pierre some time to come and find me,' Léon retorted with a shrug. 'Why didn't you tell me you were coming? I could have met you off the train in Dijon, driven you here.'

'It was a sudden decision,' she muttered, avoiding the penetrating dark stare. She wished he wasn't sitting so close to her. Against the faded blue of his workman's denim shirt his skin was Indian brown, taut across strong muscles, and he smelled not only of the soil and the vines but also of sweat. He was truly a man of the earth and exuded a strong sensuality which made her own senses quiver in response. He was so different from the men she was used to being with, the dancers and ballet-masters, the businessmen like Adrian. 'I would have been here earlier,' she went on, made nervous not only by his silence but also by the sharp physical cravings which were stabbing through her as a result of being so close to him. 'Only all sorts of things went wrong. I'll have to go back to Dijon soon to catch the train to Paris. I must be back in Paris by this evening.' She felt more confident now she had told him that and was able to look at him again. 'I came today to talk about our marital status,' she went on coolly. 'Léon, it's time we did something.'

'*Oui,*' he nodded, the sun-bleached streaked hair

sliding forward over his forehead. 'And I shall be glad to discuss it too. It has been much on my mind lately—very much.' His glance came up from studying the pattern on her dress to her face and there was something sultry in his expression which made apprehension go leaping along her nerves again. 'But it can't be discussed in an hour or so. You will have to stay for a few days.' His glance went to her foot and again he stroked the swelling with one forefinger. 'You will have to stay to rest your ankle,' he went on slowly. 'As a dancer you cannot afford to take risks with an injury like this.'

Roselle moved her foot sharply away from the caressing finger.

'I know I can't,' she said coolly. 'But I can't stay. I have to go back to Paris this evening—I promised.'

'Whom did you promise?' He slanted a sharply curious glance at her.

'A ... a friend.'

'So? We have a phone now. You could call her long-distance and tell her what has happened,' he suggested smoothly. 'Then she will not worry when you do not return, because I am not letting you go so soon, not now that you are here.'

'It isn't a question of you not letting me go. I can't stay,' she argued. 'And you can't make me stay.'

'Can't I?' he retorted. 'How little you know me, *ma chère*,' he added scoffingly. 'And how do you think you're going to get to Dijon for the train if I don't drive you there?'

'The way I came ... on the bus, of course.'

'No.' He shook his head. 'The last bus back to Dijon will pass the end of the lane in precisely five minutes, and you will not catch it because you cannot walk down the lane with a damaged ankle.'

She stared at him in consternation. He returned her stare a little mockingly.

'Then I'll have to ask Angèle ... if her brother Pierre will drive me to Dijon,' she retorted.

'Pierre has already gone home to his wife and Angèle has gone with him. She lives with them now. She comes only every other day to clean house for me.' His mouth curved in a slight smile. 'Don't bother with any more arguments, *petite*,' he said softly. 'You are staying here tonight and maybe even three or four more nights. You are staying as long as it takes to make your ankle better.'

'But I haven't brought any clothes with me,' she protested.

'I had very few with me when I came to see you in London, but I stayed,' he replied. His glance drifted down to her dress again. 'That dress is very pretty but not suitable, I admit, for the country. As for these....' he bent and picked up her flimsy sandals. '*Mon dieu*, it is no wonder you twisted your ankle!' he added dryly. 'However, there is no one here to worry about how you are dressed and you can go about barefooted in the house. So it is settled. You will stay.' He stood up. 'And now we'll have a glass of wine ... to celebrate, of course.' Over his shoulder he gave her a mocking grin as he went towards the buffet.

She was glad that he had moved away from her because it gave her a chance to collect her scattered wits. She couldn't stay with him alone in this house tonight or any other night. She must get back to Paris. But how? With Angèle gone there was no one to help her. Roselle's mouth twisted in an ironic smile. Strange that she should be thinking of asking the woman she suspected of being Léon's mistress to help her get away from him.

He came back to the couch carrying two glasses of red wine and handed one to her. Immediately she was reminded of that dark afternoon in Putney two and a half years previously.

'Is this some of your wine?' she asked, taking the glass from him.

'Yes.' He sat down close to her again on the edge of the couch. 'It is the vintage of that year I came to see you. Since then the vintages have been poor, the weather bad. But this summer perhaps I am in luck again.' He gave her a long level look and raised his glass. 'To us and the future,' he said.

Roselle looked down quickly into the ruby-red depths of the wine.

'Léon——' she began, changed her mind about what she was going to say and muttered, 'I can't drink to that.'

'Why not?'

She risked looking at him again. Sitting close to

her, his thigh pressing against hers, he was watching her with that strange sultry expression in his eyes. Her gaze faltered, wandered away from his eyes down to his mouth, and again the familiar pangs of desire twisted through her. Oh, God, why did it have to be like this? Why did he affect her like this? Why did she want to reach up, frame his face with her hands and draw it down to hers until their lips touched, until her resistance to him melted and her body arched against his, inviting invasion. Her mind suddenly aswirl with sensuousness, she gripped the glass stem hard in an attempt to hang on to cold reality. The stem snapped and the full goblet tipped over. Wine spilled like blood between them, forming a pool in her lap.

'Oh, I'm sorry!' she gasped, her glance flicking up to his.

'It seems you don't know your own strength,' he mocked. He set down his own glass quickly on the occasional table nearby, picked up the two separated pieces of the glass from her knee and then producing a large red handkerchief mopped up the pool of wine.

'I'm afraid your dress is stained for ever,' he said. 'I'll get you another glass of wine.'

'No. No ... Léon, please listen to me,' she said urgently. 'No wine and no toasts. We have to talk, sensibly....' She broke off as her attention was caught by a movement in the archway. Angèle was coming into the room and she was carrying a pair of crutches. Her fair plump face was beaming in a smile of triumph.

'Excuse me,' she said. 'Look what I have found! I knew I had seen some somewhere and Pierre reminded me that Gilles Dumay had some when he came home after breaking his leg, so I persuaded Pierre to take me over to the Dumay house to ask if we could borrow them for you, *madame*.' Angèle came across to the couch and propped the crutches against it.

'It's very kind of you to go to so much trouble,' said Roselle.

'But it has been a pleasure, *madame*, not trouble at all. I know you want to go back to Paris this evening and so I thought....'

'Madame is not going back to Paris this evening,' Léon's voice cut across Angèle's. 'She is staying here for several days, possibly for the whole summer.' Leaning against the sideboard, he folded his arms across his chest and stared at his housekeeper from under frowning eyebrows.

'Then you wish me to stay this evening to cook the dinner perhaps?' said Angèle, turning to Roselle and smiling down at her. 'It will be difficult for you to cook while your ankle is painful, *madame*. You won't be able to manage even with the crutches....'

'I shall cook the dinner.' Again Léon spoke roughly. 'Thanks for the crutches, Angèle. *Bonsoir*.'

The way he said good evening he might just as well have said 'get out', thought Roselle.

'You're sure, *madame*, you wouldn't like me to stay?' asked Angèle.

'No, she isn't sure,' said Léon. 'But I am. So be on your way, Angèle. We'll see you the day after tomorrow.'

'*Oui, monsieur.*' The woman did not seem at all put out by his autocratic manner. In fact she seemed to relish it, and Roselle wondered if being domineering herself Angèle enjoyed being dominated by a stronger personality. '*Bonsoir, madame,*' she said, smiling. 'I hope your ankle doesn't give you too much pain in the night.'

She went from the room and all was quiet again save for the singing of the birds outside the window and the tinkle of glass against glass as Léon poured wine into another goblet. He brought it to her and she began to sip it quickly before he could propose another toast. He picked up his own glass and to her relief sat down on the footstool and not beside her on the couch.

'Why doesn't Angèle live in the Château any more?' she asked after a few more moments of silence had passed.

'Who knows?' he shrugged carelessly. 'She moved to her brother's house in the village not long after I returned from London, over two years ago.' His mouth twitched humorously. 'Maybe her affection for me was getting the better of her and she found it frustrating to have to live in the same house and not share my bed,' he added. 'You see, she has always hoped to be the real *châtelaine* here. In fact she seduced Paul Arçenaut with that in mind. She hoped he would act the gentleman and marry her when she told him she was expecting his child, but instead he had a heart attack and died.' Again ironic amusement curved his mouth fleetingly. 'Then I bought the place and she turned her attentions to me.'

'You mean she hoped to conceive a child by you?' Roselle exclaimed.

'Not only hoped but is still hoping,' he replied. 'Even when I told her I was married to you and went to visit you, she did not give up.' His eyes were veiled by their thick lashes as he looked down at the empty glass in his hand. 'When I returned from London without you, she really put on the pressure,' he added softly. 'It was difficult to repulse her without losing her very competent services as a housekeeper. But somehow I managed to get the message over.' He rose to his feet and went over to pour more wine into his glass. 'She moved out, but she keeps coming back every day hoping to make herself indispensable, hoping I'll capitulate. . . .' He broke off to mutter something virulently rude about women.

'She must think it very strange that we don't live together,' Roselle remarked.

'I don't give a damn what she thinks,' he retorted.

'And she must wonder why we don't get a divorce,' she went on, testing the ground cautiously.

'She does. She has even suggested it, pointing out

to me that you do not behave as a proper wife should. You do not keep my bed warm, cook for me and keep house for me as she would.'

'I wish you'd told me all this about her that morning before you left London,' she said.

'Would it have done any good if I had? I did my best in the time available to convey to you I considered her to be unimportant,' Léon replied. Leaning against the sideboard, he drank deeply of the wine in his glass, then gave her a penetrating glance. 'You were very strange that morning. Most unreasonable.'

'Well, I like that!' she gasped. 'After reading her letter I was supposed to be reasonable?'

'In the first place you shouldn't have read a letter which was not addressed to you,' he said bitingly. 'And in the second place you had no right to make assumptions about my relationship with her.' He laughed shortly. '*Eh bien*, we are back to where we left off that day, aren't we? You were jealous and spiteful, and I still can't understand why.'

'I felt you'd deceived me, in more ways than one, and I still think you did.'

'Why?' he exclaimed. 'Because I behaved like a husband? Because I stayed and lived with you, slept with you, shared with you? That was deceiving you? And all the time I believed I was doing what you wanted, pleasing you!' He swore exasperatedly and tilted the wine bottle over his glass to fill it again. 'It seems to me you were a little guilty of deception too,' he added bitterly. He tossed off his wine, set the glass down, corked the bottle and came across to take her empty glass.

Now was the time, Roselle thought, to ask him about a divorce, now while he was angry and disliking her. She looked up, braving the darkly murderous glint in his eyes as he lingered beside the couch looking down at her.

'If that's how you feel about me you'll be glad to agree to a divorce,' she said. 'That's why I've come today—to tell you that when I return to Paris I'm going to start proceedings for one.'

'Why?'

'Why what?'

'Why do you want a divorce?' Léon sat down beside her again on the edge of the couch. Resting his forearm along the back of the couch, he leaned towards her so closely she could smell the wine on his breath, see the sheen of sweat on his face and in the hollow at the base of his throat. Cautiously and involuntarily her glance moved downwards to the froth of dark hair revealed by his unbuttoned shirt, then even farther down to his thigh across which the denim was stretched tight, and her hands itched suddenly with the desire to touch him.

She had never wanted to touch Adrian in this way. Nor any other man. Only with Léon did she feel this primitive bone-melting desire to touch intimately. But it had nothing to do with loving him, nothing at all.

'I've received a proposal of marriage,' she said stiffly.

'Only one?' he scoffed incredulously.

'What do you mean, only one?' she demanded, turning too quickly to look at him and finding only inches separated his lips from hers. She tilted her head back away from him and regarded him from beneath drooping lashes.

'I should have thought a lovely graceful woman like you who is apparently unattached would have received more than one proposal during the past couple of years,' he drawled, his glance roving avidly over the long curve of her throat. 'I've always liked that line.' His finger drifted feather-like over her skin. 'And when you tilt your head back it shows to advantage and gives me the opportunity to show my appreciation.'

His head dipped towards her. The smell of his hair filled her nostrils tantalisingly, half drugging her. His lips were warm, blazing a trail of exquisite torment, and his hand slid stealthily down to her breast, fingers seeking within the low neckline of her dress.

'No, stop it!' she cried, and thrust desperate fingers into his hair, tugging at it to pull his head up. Half gasping with pain and half laughing, Léon raised his head, seized her wrists, dragged her hands out of his hair and held them prisoner between his. Held like that the only way she could avoid his intention to plunder her mouth was to twist her head sideways and wriggle over on to her side so that she faced the back of the couch. 'Let go of me,' she panted. 'I haven't come here to make love with you.'

'Haven't you?' he mocked softly. 'Then why have you come? Not just to tell me you are thinking of starting divorce proceedings, surely. You could have done that through a lawyer.'

'I know I could.' Over her shoulder she eyed him warily and then shifted her position and tried to sit up. 'But it seemed more civilised to see you first and discuss it with you reasonably.'

'Ha!' His laugh was jeering, but his eyes were soft and sensuous as they held hers. 'Impossible for you to be reasonable,' he taunted gently, and raising both her hands to his lips he kissed them, watching her all the time. 'Impossible for me to be reasonable also, now you are here,' he continued, leaning towards her again and pressing her hands against the warmth of his chest, his eyes half closing, sultry with passion. 'As usual you intoxicate me,' he said provocatively.

'Are you sure it isn't the wine you've drunk which is doing that?' she retorted tartly, turning her head quickly again, then gasping when, finding her ear close instead of her lips, Léon bit the lobe with sharp teeth.

'I'm sure, *chérie*,' he whispered, gathering her into his arms. 'It's been a long time since we were together in London. You've been a long time coming, but now you're here I intend to make the most of your visit.'

'No!' This time Roselle used her nails, clawing at him, but not for long because he caught her hands again and twisted her arms behind her back while he laughed at her. 'Oh, I might have guessed you wouldn't play fair!' she cried. Changing her tactics, she looked up at him appealingly. 'Let me go, Léon, please let me go!'

'It's too late,' he muttered thickly. 'I can't.' And somehow he was on his feet and she was in his arms being carried across the room.

'Put me down!' she cried, pummelling him with both fists. 'Where are you taking me? What are you going to do?'

'Can't you guess?' he taunted as he carried her along the passage to a wide entrance hall, which was filled with the golden glow of the setting sun.

'I'm not going to bed with you,' she raged when he began to go up some stairs. 'I'm not!'

Calling on all her slender muscular strength developed through hours of ballet dancing, Roselle twisted and wriggled in his arms, but they merely tightened mercilessly about her and he went on up the stairs.

'Oh, this is ridiculous, going to bed at this time of the day!' she seethed sarcastically when physical objection had failed.

'I can go to bed any time of the day when it's with a woman as beautiful and tantalising as you are,' he retorted, reaching the top of the stairs and striding along a wide gallery which overlooked the main hallway.

'How can you be like this, so ... so bestial!' she stormed in powerless rage.

Léon didn't answer her and kicking open a door carried her into a low-ceilinged room which was already dusky with the purple shadows of evening. The door clicked closed. A silken bedcover rustled beneath her as he laid her on a fourposter bed. She would have rolled to the other side of the bed and off it in an attempt to escape, but she had forgotten about her ankle. Pain jagged through it agonisingly and groaning she collapsed backwards against a mound of pillows, her hair now a tangle of russet-brown waves spreading out on either side of her pale triangular face, her eyes glistening with the tears she refused to shed.

Through the blur of tears she watched Léon strip off his shirt, but when he began to slip off his trousers she averted her eyes, not wanting to see the lithe grace of his bare body, afraid of those niggling darts of desire which were stabbing through her again.

The mattress sank beneath his weight as he lounged close beside her and his fingers were warm against her skin as he loosened the drawstring which held together the bodice of her dress.

Turning her head suddenly, she looked up at the dark face looming over hers.

'I don't love you any more,' she said coldly and clearly. 'So you're wasting your time. Anything you do now will be against my will. I don't want you.'

'You've lied to me before,' he retorted, and she gasped in indignation as he began to stroke the dress from her shoulders.

'But I'm not lying. I don't love you.'

'What is love?' he jeered softly. 'Mostly wanting. You still want me—that's why you came here.'

'It isn't,' she argued, her voice coming out in a shaken whisper because his lips were tormenting the hollow at the base of her throat, moving on to tantalise the tender swell of her now half-exposed breasts and the old familiar excitement was beginning to throb through her blood.

Closing her eyes tightly so that she couldn't see him, holding her breath so that she couldn't smell the scents of his hair and skin, she willed herself to lie perfectly still and show no response. She would be as cold and as hard as a marble statue. Léon would get no satisfaction from her and then maybe he would leave her alone.

But when inevitably his lips sought hers, her mouth opened to the sweet wine taste of his sense-stirring kisses and suddenly her mind was whirling round and round, spinning faster and faster out of control. Her heart was racing, thundering in her ears, and her body was tautening until she felt she would explode with the agony of desire.

'Help me, oh, help me,' she moaned and turned to him, reaching to enfold him in her urgent arms, luxuriating in the feel of his hard smooth shoulders against the palms of her hands.

'With pleasure, *ma chérie*.' His voice, slightly breathless, mocked her and he gathered her close to him.

As the heat of his passion developed and invaded her, spreading through her, all the pressures which had built up within her while they had been separated were released. For a few moments she knew a wild sublime ecstasy as the love she had always felt for him broke through the doors which she had closed on it and surged up in a burst of uncontrollable joy. Then she was sighing and sagging against him and the tears which she had held back for so long were sliding down her cheeks, wetting his chest as he held her closely, not saying anything but stroking her hair, her cheek and her throat until, soothed and comforted, she drifted off to sleep.

CHAPTER FOUR

'ROSELLE!' Her name was a soft sibilance wooing her from the depths of sleep, coaxing her to the surface of full consciousness. So many times she had dreamed she had heard Léon speaking to her like that, calling her gently yet teasingly as if he were very amused by her, so she opened her eyes hopefully, only to find he hadn't been there and that she had slept alone.

She wasn't going to open her eyes now. She was going to keep them closed and try to fall asleep again, because in sleep there was no pain, no regret for what might have been, no wishful thinking.

'Roselle!' This time the voice was crisper. It commanded, and she smiled as she turned her head on the pillow, enjoying that note of mastery when it was addressed to herself.

'Yes?' she whispered.

'You've slept a long time, almost twelve hours, just like a baby, and it's seven o'clock in the morning and time you had something to eat.

Morning? Her eyes flew open. She wasn't dreaming, then. Léon was there, actually there, sitting on the side of the bed close beside her, fully dressed in clean denims. He had shaved and his hair was damp and smooth, pale as straw where it had been bleached by the hot Burgundian sun. But his eyes were, as ever, dark as the devil's, slightly slanted and mysterious above the high sun-tanned cheekbones. Behind him, yellow as butter, sunlight slanted in through a half-opened lattice window, gleaming on antique chests of drawers and causing the gold threads in the red silk damask of the bed hangings to glitter.

'Oh! What happened?' she gasped, freeing an arm from the confines of the soft fleecy blanket which covered her and pushing back tangled hair from her sleep-flushed face. Underneath the blanket she was completely naked, she realised, and with that realisation came the memory of the ecstasy she had experienced with him the previous night and she was flooded suddenly with a sense of shame at her own weakness where he was concerned. 'Oh, I'll never forgive you,' she wailed. 'Never!' And turning over she buried her face in the damask-covered pillows.

'Never forgive me for what?' he asked coolly.

'For what happened. For what you did last night,' she replied, her voice muffled.

'There is nothing to forgive,' he argued calmly. 'What happened, what I did and you did, was a normal part of marriage. It was the culmination of our feelings for each other, an expression of the emotions we experienced on meeting again after so long a separation.'

The mocking inflection in the quietly reasonable voice grated on her nerves and she flung over to glare at him.

'Feelings? All you felt was ... was lust!' She spat the words at him, noticing that his narrowed gaze was lingering fervently on her bare creamy-skinned shoulders before sliding down to her breasts which were just showing above the edge of the blanket. Ostentatiously she pulled the blanket right up to her chin and leaned back against the headboard to stare at him haughtily. Amusement glinted in the dark eyes as they met hers again.

'So,' he shrugged. 'I agree, there was something of that in the way I felt. You have grown very beautiful, as I guessed you would one day, and I lost control.' Heavy eyelids hid his eyes and that slight secretive smile which always tormented her so much curved his mouth. 'But what of yourself, *chérie?* How would you describe what you felt yesterday evening? I'm sure lust is too masculine a word to describe a woman's sexual desire.'

'I felt nothing,' she said between gritted teeth.

'*Vraiment?*' Now his glance was wickedly derisive. 'But I would never have believed it,' he went on with mocking surprise. 'You must have developed into a very good actress. Your kisses were so ardent, your caresses so arousing that they increased my desire, and I could have sworn you felt the same way I did. In fact I have been thinking this morning how fortunate I am to have such a passionate wife. Many men would envy me.'

'I wouldn't have ... I mean, it wouldn't have happened if you hadn't forced yourself upon me.' Her lips trembled in spite of her efforts to remain calm and collected and with a little moan of irritation she turned her face away from him. 'I hate you!' she whispered viciously. 'I hate you, and I wish I hadn't come to see you.'

'You'll get over feeling like that,' he said imperturbably. 'I expect it will take you a while to adjust, but after you have been here for a few days. . . .'

'I am not staying here for a few days!' she seethed, turning to glare at him again. 'I'm going back to Paris today to have my ankle examined by an orthopaedic surgeon.'

'You could have that done in Lyon,' he replied.

'I prefer to have it treated by a specialist I know and in whom I have confidence,' she retorted defiantly.

'You know of one in Paris?' he queried conversationally.

'Yes. He's treating Anya Merimée.' And she went on to tell him about Anya's accident and how as the ballerina's understudy she had achieved her own ambition to dance the part of Giselle. And Léon listened as he had always listened to her, his dark glance steady on her face yet expressing nothing of what he might be thinking or feeling.

'So at last you are no longer too innocent or too lacking in emotional experience to be able to interpret such a part,' he murmured slowly when she had finished. His eyes narrowed assessingly. 'It would seem you have grown up,' he remarked dryly. 'At last.'

Something flickered in her memory. She had a sudden image of him five years ago, staring at her with fever-bright eyes and saying, 'Little Roselle, when are you going to grow up?'

'Of course I've grown up,' she retorted. 'And now that I've shown I can dance one leading role I'll probably be offered more. That's why I don't want to take any risks with my ankle. Léon, please will you take me to Dijon this morning so I can catch the train to Paris. I should be able to manage on the crutches.'

His face impassive, he studied her once more with narrowed eyes, then with a quick movement he flicked aside the blanket to reveal her long narrow dancer's feet.

'The swelling isn't any worse,' he murmured, stroking her left ankle with one long forefinger, and at once she pulled her foot away.

'Don't touch me! I don't like you to touch me,' she said tautly.

'You like it,' he replied with a grin. 'But you don't like to admit that you do.' He twitched the blanket back over her foot and stood up. 'It's time I started work,' he said, and began to walk round the end of the bed towards the door.

'Then you won't drive me into Dijon this morning?' she demanded, sitting up urgently and clutching the blanket about her.

'No, not this morning. I'm too busy.' He stopped at the end of the bed and looked down its length at her. 'It would be best if you rest here, *ma mie*, while you can,' he added softly. 'The longer you rest your ankle the sooner it will get better. I told your friend —the one you should have phoned last night—that that is what you would be doing for the next few days.'

'My ... my friend?' she stammered. She had forgotten all about Adrian. She had been too sunk in a passion-induced sleep last night to phone him.

'*Oui.* He phoned late last night wanting to know what had happened to you and why you hadn't phoned him.'

'He?' she quavered croakily, made suddenly nervous by the way Léon was looking at her from under severely frowning eyebrows.

'He said he was Adrian Corwell.'

'Then why didn't you wake me so I could speak to him?' she blustered, to cover her nervousness.

'I had tried once to wake you, but you were too deeply asleep even to have some supper with me, so I thought it best to leave you.'

He shrugged his broad shoulders and half turned away from the bed as if to go towards the door again. 'Your friend seemed to understand when I told him that I hesitated to disturb you just to bring you downstairs to the phone because you had hurt your ankle. He agreed with me that you should rest it as much as possible.' He slanted her a curious glance. 'Does he have something to do with the ballet company you dance with?'

'No. But he is a balletomane.' She saw him look puzzled and went on to explain quickly, 'He's a ballet fan and attends as many performances as possible and tries to interest other people in the art. He's a businessman of some sort. I think he holds shares in several companies and sits on their boards.'

'So he's wealthy?'

'Very.'

'And has plenty of time to go chasing ballet dancers, I suppose,' he suggested with a sneer. 'He seemed very anxious about you. That's why I wondered if he belonged to the ballet.' He turned to face her, his eyes as sharp as daggers seeming to stab right into hers. 'Is he your lover?' he asked curtly.

'No, he isn't,' she retorted. 'I've told you before, I don't have lovers—I'm not like that. Did he leave a message for me?'

'He said he had to come by this way on Friday when he would be driving down to the Riviera. He said he would like to call in to see you, so I agreed. That's all.'

Roselle stared at him in consternation. Adrian was coming here, would be here tomorrow. He and

Léon were going to meet after all, and there didn't seem to be anything she could do to stop the meeting. Unless she could phone Adrian before he left Paris and arrange to meet him in Dijon or Mâcon or some other town—if she could get out of Montenay.

'Léon, before Adrian comes we must talk,' she said urgently.

'About what?' He folded his bare brawny forearms across his chest, his whole attitude so intimidating that she hesitated again. 'About our marital status?' he added jeeringly.

'Yes. Adrian wants to marry me.' She blurted it out.

'Aha!' Derision curled his long mouth. 'So he is the one who has proposed. Then I wish him luck, for he is going to find it very difficult to marry you since you are already married to me.' The dark eyes were insolent now as their gaze flicked over her. 'I presume you have told him.'

'Of course I have, and it didn't make any difference to him. He still wants to marry me.' Her gaze faltered, avoiding the penetration of Léon's and flicking away to the window, to the summer-blue sky she could see through it. 'I'd like to be free of our arrangement,' she said in a hard flat voice, wondering why she felt as if she were being torn apart inside when she spoke the words.

'Don't you mean Olga Valenska's arrangement?'

The quiet voice held an edge which rasped her taut nerves.

'Oh, whatever you like to call it,' she snapped irritably. 'Will you agree to a divorce?'

Léon didn't answer at once and she ventured a glance in his direction, but he wasn't looking at her. His arms still folded across his chest, he was staring at the end of the bed, and frowning.

'On what grounds?' he asked at last.

'I ... er ... don't know.' She was flustered by the question, mostly because she had expected him to come out with a firmly spoken negative answer. 'But it shouldn't be too hard for us to get one.'

'Shouldn't it?' He looked at her. 'What makes you think that?'

'Well, we haven't lived together except for those two months in London. We've never really lived together as husband and wife.'

'That's true,' he conceded slowly. 'But that is only because you haven't had the time—to be a wife, I mean. You've always been too busy with your career to come here and live with me as my wife. I realise it is something you have had to do and that's why I've never insisted you come here. You had to come here of your own free will, or not at all.'

'Oh, I don't understand why you've stayed married to me if you'd wanted a wife like that,' she flared stormily. 'You don't love me, you've never loved me. You married me only for that money. I know you did, no matter what you say about being ill at the time and not knowing what you were doing. You weren't delirious when you said "I will."'

'I married you because my grandmother arranged it,' he retorted coldly, his eyes beginning to glint with anger. 'But you're right. Love didn't enter into it and I have never pretended it did ... like you have.'

'I didn't pretend I was in love with you,' Roselle gasped in outrage. 'I *was* in love with you. I wouldn't have agreed to marry you if I hadn't been. Nor would I have let you stay with me in London. But if you'd loved me you'd have stayed until the ballet season was over....'

'You'd have liked that, wouldn't you?' he interrupted jeeringly. 'You like having a man trailing about after you ... like this Adrian Corwell does. You like having one sitting at home waiting for you, ready to lick your hands and wag his tail ... like a tame poodle.' His voice thickened in disgust. '*Mon dieu*, after two months of living like that I had had enough,' he added tautly. 'I am not tame, and you should know that by now. I go my own way. But there was nothing to stop you from coming here any time you wanted when you weren't dancing. You're welcome to stay now, to live here as long as you want....'

'As long as I don't get in your way, I suppose,' she cried out, hurt beyond bearing by his denigration of that time they had had together in London, which for her had been romance come true. 'As long as I take second place to your obsession, Montenay. As long as I submit to your desires and put up with having your mistress as a housekeeper!'

'Angèle is not and never has been my mistress, and even if she were or had been it's none of your concern, as I've told you before,' he retorted. 'I explained about her yesterday and I thought you understood.'

'But you didn't deny that you and she have been intimate at some time,' she accused shakily. 'And ... and for all I know you could have another mistress by now.'

'You're right, I could,' he countered exasperatedly. 'So why don't you stay for a while and find out, you suspicious bitch?'

'You don't have to call me names,' she objected hotly.

'I'm only getting my own back on you,' he grated. 'You've accused me of some nasty traits of character. Last night I was bestial because I wanted to make love to you ... my wife. This morning you've accused me of lust and adultery.'

He was paler than she had ever seen him. Bone gleamed whitely along the line of his jaw as he set his teeth and his eyes glowed with that murderous glint she had seen before. It seemed to her that the whole room vibrated with his anger.

He moved suddenly, swinging to stride towards the door. There he stopped to look back at her.

'This talk which you wanted to have so much is

getting us nowhere, and I have no more time to spare for it this morning,' he said curtly.

'All you have to do is say you'll agree to a divorce and let me leave today to go back to Paris,' Roselle said tonelessly. 'Oh, Léon, you must see we can't go on like this. You said once we have nothing in common, and you were right,' she added miserably.

'But I can't agree to a divorce, at least not yet,' he said, coming back into the room.

'Why not?'

'I can't afford one,' he said flatly.

'Oh, that's ridiculous!' she said scornfully, glancing round the room, seeing in the decorations the expense he had gone to. 'You must have made some money in the past two years, made a profit from the sale of wine and cattle.'

'Not enough,' he replied coolly. 'And as I told you, the last two vintages were failures. The wine was poor. Then I have had to re-invest any profits in the land. I don't have enough money in the bank to pay back that money which Olga gave me which she called your dowry and which should have been left to you.'

'You don't have to pay it back,' she said, staring at him in bewilderment.

'No? It seems, *ma chère*, you haven't read the marriage contract we signed too well. It says quite clearly that in case of our marriage failing I have to return the dowry to you. Apparently that was normal practice in the old days when arranged marriages were more common. I have consulted a lawyer on the matter already and he says there is no way I can get out of complying with that clause, since I obviously agreed to it when I signed the contract.'

Roselle stared at him in silence, absorbing the sense of what he had said. If he had consulted a lawyer he must have been considering divorce. Why? So he could marry Angèle? Or was there some other woman hovering in the background?

'I ... I ... wouldn't insist that you pay it to me,' she muttered, avoiding his glance.

'Wouldn't you? That's generous of you, *petite*,' he said dryly. 'But I'm quite sure your lawyer would insist, and also perhaps this man Corwell.' He began to walk towards the door again and paused in midstride to look back at her again. 'You know, it's a good thing he is coming this way tomorrow and I'll have a chance to meet him. I'll be able to judge whether he'll make a more suitable husband for you than I am.'

'But you have no right to do that!' she exclaimed, sitting up straight on the bed, still clutching the blanket about her.

'I think I have,' he retorted arrogantly. 'When my grandmother arranged our marriage she made me responsible for you whether you like it or not, and I have always taken my responsibilities seriously.'

'No, you haven't. You've never taken me seriously.' Roselle accused furiously. 'You've just made the most of the situation as you found it.'

'Is there any other way to live?' he remarked cynically.

'And that's what you're doing now!'

'*C'est vrai*,' he shrugged.

'But you have no right to decide whether Adrian will make me a better husband than you are. Only I have the right to do that, and I'd like to be free to consider his proposal.'

'In that case you have time to wait for me to meet him before I come to a definite decision about a divorce. And you will stay here until he comes to-morrow.'

Across the room his eyes challenged her and her mind rocked. If she stayed another night with him, if she slept another night in this bed with him. . . . A dangerous heat swept through her.

'I'm not staying!' she almost shouted at him, but he had gone from the room and she was only talking to herself.

For a few moments she sat there, upright on the bed, listening to the soft sound of Léon's footsteps on the bare wooden floor of the gallery as he went along it. Then with a groan of vexation she flung herself down on her stomach and punched at the pillows with one fist. The quarrel with him had churned up her insides and now she was hurting in the way he had always been able to make her hurt by not saying what she wanted to hear.

She flung on to her back and gazed about the

room. It had been decorated fairly recently. Ivory walls gleamed with new paint, a pale background for the rich wine and gold draperies and glossy antique furniture. A thick-piled carpet covered the floor. The whole room was surprisingly luxurious and yet she supposed that at one time the whole house had been like this when the Chauvigny family had been wealthy and the wines of Château Montenay had been famous.

It would be pleasant to stay in this room all day, to use her injured ankle as an excuse to lie in the comfortable bed and idle the hours away until Léon came in from supervising the work in the vineyard and the rest of the estate; to wait for his return like a wife, safe in the knowledge that she was welcome to stay as long as she wanted to.

She drifted off into a day-dream imagining herself as the real *châtelaine* of the Château. She would take on the management of the lovely old house, continue with the restoration of it. She would entertain in it, organise wine-tastings, make Montenay famous again throughout Burgundy, throughout France. She would bring up children in it, hers and Léon's children, dainty black-eyed girls and lively russet-haired boys.

The dream faded. How could she stay here and have Léon's children when she knew he didn't love her? Last evening there had been nothing loving about their coming together—at least she didn't think so. He had wanted her and he had *made* her want him. It had been an eruption of earthy passion only, and that was not enough on which to base a good complete marriage. There had to be something else, some spiritual feeling, and Léon didn't have that sort of feeling for her. He had said he didn't.

But Adrian loved her and had said so. Adrian had followed her about Europe. Léon's remark about a tame poodle leapt into her mind and she was tempted to giggle, but the next instant she banished the thought as being unkind. Adrian wasn't like a poodle. He made her feel special and he was going to come tomorrow, to rescue her and whisk her off to his villa at Cap d'Antibes.

If only he were more physically attractive to her! If only he were not so old. If only she didn't feel as if she were out with a kind indulgent uncle when she was lunching or dining with him. If only he were young, vibrant and tantalising ... like Léon.

She writhed on the bed. What was she going to do now? How was she going to forget last night? How was she going to obliterate from her mind the feel of sinewy sun-browned limbs twining with hers and the pressure of long fingers, with magic in their tips, seeking and finding the hidden places which gave her so much pleasure? How was she going to shut out the sound of Léon's voice, soft and slightly breathless with passion weaving spells of sensuousness about her? How could she rub from her lips the sweet wildness of his kisses silencing her answering sighs and moans of desire . . . ?

'Bonjour, madame.'

The high-pitched female voice with the rolling Burgundian accent was jarring. It shattered Roselle's sensual fantasy as a hard stone shatters a window pane. She raised her head to glare indignantly at Angèle, who, unaware of the hostility which was being silently directed at her, moved towards the bedside table and set down the breakfast tray she had brought. 'Have you slept well, madame?' she asked, and her broad-cheeked pink-skinned face beamed cheerfully.

'Yes, thank you.' Roselle was suddenly very conscious of her tangled hair, of the creased bedcover on top of which she was lying and most of all of her nudity under the folds of the blanket. Angèle's brown bovine eyes missed nothing and even now were roving over the bed with avid curiosity.

'I have brought you some hot chocolate and some fresh rolls and confiture,' Angèle said. 'If you would like to sit up, madame, I'll put the tray across your knees.'

'No, thank you. Please leave the tray where it is. I'll help myself,' replied Roselle, wondering how she could get the woman to go without being actually rude to her.

'It's a lovely morning,' Angèle went on in her garrulous way. Dressed in another simple sleeveless blouse and gathered cotton skirt, which did nothing to make her look slimmer than she was, her luxuriant hair glowing in the sunlight, her burnished skin shining with good health, she was beautiful in a countrified way; a big bouncing Burgundian woman full of good cheer and *joie de vivre*. 'Is there anything else I can get for you?' she asked generously.

'My handbag, please. I think I must have left it in the *salon*—oh, and the crutches. I'll need them when I get up. I have to get up and go downstairs to make a telephone call.'

'I'll go and get them,' said Angèle agreeably, and left the room.

Roselle waited until she could hear the woman going down the stairs, then she swung off the bed and hopped over to one of the chests of drawers. After pulling open a couple of the drawers she found one containing what she was looking for, some of Léon's shirts neatly ironed and folded, laundered no doubt, she thought rather waspishly, by the competent Angèle. She took one, shook it out and pulled it over her head. Made from crisp cotton patterned in brown, it covered her nudity more than adequately and she had to turn back the sleeves.

The sound of floorboards creaking under heavy footsteps heralded Angèle's return upstairs. But by the time she came in through the door Roselle was sitting up in bed with the breakfast tray across her knees and was drinking the delicious hot creamy chocolate.

'Here you are,' Angèle panted, and placed the

handbag on the bed and propped the crutches
against a chair.

'Thank you very much. It's very kind of you. But
please don't stay.'

'I'll wait until you have finished with the tray,
madame, then you won't have to struggle with it,'
replied Angéle imperturbably, her bright glance
taking in the shirt and then slanting sideways to the
drawer in the chest which in her haste Roselle had
left carelessly open. Going over to the chest, Angèle
pushed the drawer closed. Then bending, she lifted
something from the floor near the bed.

'Your dress, *madame*,' she said. 'It is creased with
lying there all night. Ah, *tiens*, and what a stain
there is on it!'

'Yes, I'm afraid I spilt some wine on it last night,'
said Roselle tautly. 'Please put it on the chair.'

'But wouldn't you like me to wash it for you?'
Angèle examined the label inside the neckline. ' It
is washable,' she added, 'and it will soon dry in the
sunshine.'

'No, thank you. You see, I'll have to wear it—I
didn't bring any other clothes. Could you take the
tray now, please. I've finished.'

'But of course, *madame*.' Angèle came forward
and lifted the tray on to the bedside table. 'I'll
bring you the crutches,' she said. '*Monsieur le patron* has adjusted them, I think,' she went on, 'and
they should be the right size.'

She leaned the crutches against the bed near

Roselle but made no attempt to go away.

'Would you like me to draw the water for a bath, *madame*?' she asked. 'The bathroom is right there, through that door. *Le patron* said that this room had to have its own bathroom when he began to renovate it last autumn. You like this room? He worked very hard on decorating it. He did it all himself—except for the draperies, of course.'

'Yes, yes ... It's very nice,' said Roselle, hanging on to her patience with an effort. 'But I'll manage the bath by myself. It's kind of you to want to wait on me, but I'm sure you have enough to do already.' Either Angèle was very thick-skinned or she didn't understand plain French when it was spoken, because she just stood there smiling angelically and nodding her head, making no move to go. 'And what about your little boy?' Roselle went on in another attempt to get the woman to leave the room. 'Mightn't he be getting into mischief while you're up here?'

'You're right, *madame*, he might,' agreed Angèle placidly. 'But he isn't with me this morning. I don't bring him any more because he is a little devil.' She rolled her big eyes. 'You wouldn't believe the things he has done when my back has been turned! I am at my wits' end wondering how to cope with him.'

'How old is he?' asked Roselle.

'Just five.'

'And where is he now?'

'I leave him with my sister-in-law, Bernice, Pierre's wife. He plays with his cousins while I work here.' Angèle let out a deep dragging sigh. 'He needs a father, that one, someone with authority who can control him. It is necessary that I marry soon, I think, to provide him with a father.'

'Oh?' Roselle was surprised and showed it. 'Do you have anyone in mind?'

'I had.' Again Angèle sighed deeply and the glance which she gave Roselle was strangely reproachful. 'But unfortunately it turned out that he was married already although his wife didn't live with him.'

'I see.' Roselle spoke croakily, realising that Angèle was referring to Léon. 'Yes, that ... that is unfortunate for you.' She picked fluff absently from the blanket as she considered an idea which flashed into her mind. 'Angèle, I have to go back to Paris today, this morning in fact,' she said quickly. 'But Léon says he doesn't have the time to drive me to Bezalay to get the bus back to Dijon so I can catch a train. It seems he's too busy in the vineyard.'

'But of course he is busy this time of the year,' said Angèle rather severely as if she were a teacher speaking to an ignorant pupil. 'This is the important time for the vines when the tiny grapes are growing and I know *le patron* likes to watch over them closely. A hundred days it takes after the blossoms have appeared for the grapes to reach full maturity. That will be in late September and then we shall have the *vendange* and all of us will go picking grapes. Ah, that is a great time, *madame*. We work hard in the sunshine, but we have fun too. You should be here for that.'

'I would like to be ... some time,' said Roselle. 'But today I must leave. I must get back to Paris. You see, it's most important that I see a specialist about my ankle. I'm very worried about it. It must be treated properly so I can continue my career as a dancer. I'm sure you understand that.'

'Yes, I do, *madame*. It comes first with you in the same way that his work comes first with *le patron*,' said Angèle. 'But what I do not understand is why you are married to him if you prefer to dance in the ballet. How can you be a proper wife if you are a dancer?'

There was a note of censure in the woman's voice which roused Roselle's independent spirit, but on looking at the broad pink cheeks and placid brown eyes she decided it was impossible for her to even attempt to explain to Angèle how the ways of the world, far away from this small village in Burgundy, had changed, and that many women were able to carry on careers and be wives as well. To do that would only cause an argument and at the moment she didn't want to antagonise Angèle. On the contrary, she wanted the woman's help.

'You admire *le patron* very much, don't you?' she said softly.

'Ah, *oui*. What woman wouldn't admire a man

like him?' Angèle's sincerity was almost embarrass-
ing. 'He is so strong and ambitious, so masterful. *Il
est beau comme un tigre*,' she added, her eyes shining as she made her confession of adoration.

Her frankness was shattering, Roselle found.
Beautiful as a tiger. She couldn't have described
Léon more aptly herself. Lithely muscular, amber-
haired, tawny-skinned and black-eyed, he had the
inscrutable detachment of the jungle cat, possessed
an aloofness which both challenged and enticed,
and Angèle was attracted to him as much as she was.
Or rather as much as she had been once, she corrected herself hastily.

But the correction came too late to stop jealousy
from needling through her sharply. She was jealous
because Angèle had lived close to Léon ever since
he had come to Montenay. Angèle had seen him
almost every day, in fact, and had been able to do
some of the things a wife usually does for her husband. And with the jealousy came a raw shocking
desire to reach up and scratch out Angèle's eyes
because they had admired and coveted Léon's masculine attractions.

'Since you feel like that about him, I'm sure you
would be willing to help him,' she said stiltedly,
forcing herself to be pleasant.

'*Oui, madame*, I would do anything for him,'
said Angèle fervently. 'If you knew how kind he
was to me when he first came here you wouldn't be
surprised that I admire him so much,' she added

as if she had realised how strange it might seem to her employer's wife that his housekeeper admired him. ' I had just had the baby and when Monsieur Arçenaut died I didn't know where to turn for help. I thought I would lose my job here when the new owner came. But Monsieur Chauvigny let me stay on.'

'Yes, he told me about that,' said Roselle between her teeth, still trying to put down the jealousy she was feeling.

'So will you tell me what it is I can do for you that would help him?' asked Angèle.

'You can ask your brother to drive me to Bezalay to catch the next bus for Dijon. I presume there is one going from there this morning?'

'*Oui*, there is, *madame*, but it has already left. You would be better off going to Tournus,' replied the practical woman. 'But *le patron* said you would be staying for a few days.'

'Never mind what he said. He was being kind again, as you know he can be. But he doesn't really want me here and I can't stay. I must go back to Paris. Please will you ask Pierre to drive me to Tournus, then?'

'I can't. Pierre isn't at work this morning. He is sick.' Angèle's eyes flashed angrily. 'Ah, he is a typical Arçenaut! He drinks too much wine, just like Monsieur Paul used to do. Then he is ill and can't work. *Monsieur le patron* has threatened to sack him many times for drinking too much.'

'Did you walk here from the village this morning?' asked Roselle, feeling defeated by the information when she had believed that she had solved the problem of leaving Montenay without asking Léon again to drive her.

'No. I should not be here this morning,' confided Angèle guiltily. 'But I guessed you might need some help, *madame*, so I drove here in Pierre's truck.'

'You can drive?' Roselle couldn't hide her surprise.

'Of course I can.' Angèle looked smug. 'I drive the truck often. Pierre taught me and now I drive better than he does.' She paused, then added suggestively, 'I could drive you to Tournus, if you wish.'

For a moment Roselle studied the bland pink-cheeked face, the suspicion crossing her mind that Angèle was very eager to help her leave Montenay, eager to get rid of le patron's wife possibly because she wanted him all to herself.

'I would do it of course, to help *le patron* so that he doesn't have to stop in the middle of his work to drive you,' Angèle added humbly.

'Thank you. I'm very grateful and I expect he will be too when he knows you have helped me,' said Roselle.

'Then I'll go and bring the truck round to the kitchen entrance now and then I'll come back to help you down the stairs,' said Angèle, taking the tray from the bedside table.

Over half an hour later, still a little uneasy over

the woman's willingness to help her, Roselle sat next to Angèle in front of the truck as it lurched at high speed along the narrow poplar-edged lane towards the road. All about them the green countryside shimmered in the bright morning sunlight. Down in the river valley cattle grazed lush meadows. On the higher slopes the rows of vines were neat and straight, giving the land a severely tailored look. In the distance thick forests were a bluish-green blur on the gentle curves of the hills and beyond them the far-off mountains of Jura glowed with faint violet light against the eastern sun-bright sky.

Through the small village of Montenay the truck trundled. The old houses, the colours of their walls as rich and varied in colour as the wines which the region produced, clustered together round the small square, their tiled roofs vivid splashes of orange. In front of the truck hens ran clucking and some women who were standing about talking at an open doorway turned to wave to Angèle, who shouted something to them through the open window as she passed.

Angèle was not a bad driver, but she did have a tendency to drive in the middle of the road and several times on that journey Roselle found herself closing her eyes and wincing when they swung round a bend, convinced they were going to meet another vehicle coming the other way in a head-on crash. But there was little traffic on the country road which swooped across the Burgundain countryside to the town of Tournus, and they made good time, arriving in the medieval town with its massive Abbey and winding narrow streets just as the bus from Dijon arrived to unload its passengers and turn around for the return journey to the capital of the province.

True to her generous and over-affectionate nature Angèle went with Roselle to the bus, carrying her handbag for her while she hobbled along on the crutches, even coming on to the bus to make sure she was settled comfortably in a seat near a window. Or to make sure she really left, thought Roselle, with another twinge of suspicion.

'And when will you be coming back, *madame*?' asked Angèle pleasantly enough.

'You would be glad if I never came back, wouldn't you?' Roselle said challengingly, and Angèle's big brown eyes widened.

'*Comment*? I do not understand,' she said.

'I know Léon is the man you would have liked to be your husband and act as a father to your little boy. You would still like him for a husband, wouldn't you?'

'Ah, *mon dieu*, what can I say?' exclaimed Angèle. 'It is a dream I have, nothing more, a romantic dream.' A guarded anxious look came into her eyes. 'But I wouldn't like to be named as the third party in any divorce case, *madame*,' she whispered urgently. 'I have my reputation to think of. That is why I moved out of the Château when I found out he was still married to you and had not been able to get an annulment that time he went to see you in London. The people in the village were beginning to talk about him and me.' Angèle's eyes were covered by their heavy lids as she looked down at her big capable hands as they clasped each other. 'The way of the world is cruel, *n'est-ce pas, madame*?' she said quietly.

'What do you mean?'

'In the way that some people who should not be married to each other are married to each other and how others who should be married to each other are not.' The heavy eyes lifted and the brown eyes were no longer smiling or surprised. Their expression was truly vindictive. 'I would make *le patron* a much better wife than you, *madame*, and for that reason I say to you, yes, I shall be glad if you never come back. *Au revoir, madame.*'

She turned and bustled down the aisle between the seats, pausing to make some sort of earthy remark to the driver, who roared with laughter. The last Roselle saw of her as the bus moved away was the beam of her smile and the sheen of her thick golden brown hair and pink skin as she waved goodbye.

In contrast to the journey of the previous day the return journey to Paris went smoothly and quickly. The bus arrived at Dijon station in time for Roselle to catch the next train, which met with no delays and reached Paris two and a half hours later.

Even so she had plenty of time for introspection, to think about the situation between herself and Léon, to ponder on Angèle's remarks and to wonder what she was going to say to Adrian when she saw him.

She would have to tell him she couldn't give him an answer to his proposal yet because Léon could not agree to a divorce. He would be annoyed, she guessed, but that couldn't be helped. Possibly it would make him change his mind about wanting to marry her. In a way she hoped it would, because she had learned something during her visit to Montenay. She had learned that she didn't want to marry him.

As soon as she arrived in Paris she took a taxi to the hospital where Anya had been treated and although she wasn't able to see Dr Messange, the orthopaedic surgeon who specialised in dealing with injuries sustained by dancers, her ankle was X-rayed and an appointment was made for her to see him next day.

From the hospital she went to her apartment. To her surprise Cécile, her apartment mate, was at home and equally surprised to see her.

'What are you doing here?' exclaimed the vivacious dark-eyed, dark-haired French girl. 'You're supposed to be somewhere in Burgundy. Your friend Monsieur Corwell was here and told me so. . . .'

'Adrian was here?' Roselle interrupted her, sink-ing down on to the nearest chair. 'Why? What did he want?'

'He asked me to pack some of your clothes. He said he was going to meet you in Burgundy, at a place called Montenay, I think he said.'

'He was, but not until tomorrow.'

'He said he was going today. He was all worked up, worried and excited. He must be nearly there by now. He said you had hurt your ankle and couldn't come back here for your clothes to take to the Riviera, so he would take them to you.' Cécile looked comically puzzled. 'But you are back,' she said, and made a helpless gesture with both hands. 'I give up! I never was good at guessing. You are here and he is half way there.'

'But how could he leave Paris today? He said he had meetings all day.'

'He told me he had decided not to go to them.' Cécile began to laugh. 'Oh, imagine, Roselle, his face when he gets there and finds you have left and have come back here! He's going to be so angry!'

'Yes, I'm afraid he is.' Roselle was laughing too, quite helplessly, but not at Adrian. She was laughing at herself and her own futile efforts to prevent him and Léon from meeting.

CHAPTER FIVE

THE night was hot, so hot that it was necessary to have every window in the small apartment open, with the result that the sound of traffic passing by in the street several storeys below invaded the rooms, especially the bedroom where Roselle usually slept.

Not that she was anywhere near sleeping, she thought, as she lay on her back in the darkness. She was too disturbed, wondering what had happened at Montenay when Adrian had arrived there; trying to guess what he and Léon had said to each other.

And where was Adrian now? Why hadn't he phoned her when he had found out she had returned to Paris? Perhaps he would phone in the morning. Perhaps he was driving back here even now, through the night. Perhaps Léon had liked him and had decided that he would make her a better husband than himself. . . .

She turned restlessly, not liking that thought, not wanting to face up to it, and closing her eyes imagined she was back in the lovely ivory-walled bedroom at Montenay which Léon had renovated and decorated himself. A cool country breeze scented with roses and wild flowers wafted through the open latticed window. It was early evening, that quiet time of lavender-coloured light, and the moon was a silvery-gold sickle hanging outside the window. Roselle could see it through her lashes as she lay in the wide four-poster bed and drifted into deep contented slumber while someone stroked her hair, her cheek, her throat....

A bell shrilled and all the nerves in her body jumped, startling her into wakefulness. She opened her eyes to brilliant sunshine flooding the small apartment room which had cooled only slightly during the night. Through the open window came the sound of morning traffic and the noise of radios blaring out from other apartments. The slightly open door was pushed open further and Cécile appeared, her abundant black hair straggling down about her shoulders, her slim body gleaming whitely through the thin gauze of her shift-like nightgown.

'Telephone ... for you,' she said.

'Adrian?' queried Roselle, swinging her legs out of bed and cautiously putting her weight on both feet. The left ankle was still slightly swollen, but there was no sharp pain.

'No, René,' replied Cécile, coming over to her with the crutches. 'I've told him about the injury to your ankle, so be prepared to be blasted for carelessness!'

True to character, the director of the Ballet

Godin made some extremely rude remarks about Roselle being stupid enough to go walking along country roads in high-heeled shoes, then asked more calmly,

'Have you been to see Dr Messange about it?'

'I have an appointment to see him today at eleven o'clock.'

'Good. I shall meet you at his office in the hospital. I want to talk to you.'

'What about?'

'You'll find out. Just be prepared to spend the day with me. I'm going to take you to see a friend of mine.'

'But René, I'm expecting....' Roselle protested.

'Cancel any other plans you have made for today,' he said at his most autocratic and ballet-master manner. 'If you want to further your career as a ballerina you will do as I say.'

'*Oui, monsieur,*' she replied automatically, and rang off.

Lean, dark and dynamic, with a neat pointed beard and curly black hair, he was waiting as he had promised outside Dr Messange's office when she hobbled out.

'So what is the verdict?' he demanded. 'Am I to lose the services of another good ballerina?'

'No,' she replied with a smile. 'He says that as soon as the swelling has died down I can begin to exercise it a little each day. Meanwhile I have to go about on the crutches and rest it as much as possible. Nothing is broken. I've sprained a ligament. that's all. It's painful but not irreparable.'

'Thank God for that,' he said, putting his arm about her shoulders and giving her a quick affectionate hug, 'because I have great things planned for you in the autumn when the theatre season starts again. But right now we're going to drive out to Barbizon to have lunch with Anton Charron. You've heard of him, perhaps.'

'Doesn't he make films? Documentaries for the television?'

'That is so. But I'll explain more when we're in the car.'

He drove his small Peugeot with the same energy with which he directed a ballet on the stage, weaving in and out of the stream of traffic which was drawn as if by a magnet towards the Etoile, that huge roundabout dominated by the Arc de Triomphe, the symbol of France, and as he drove he talked fast, using his hands in many gestures, often taking both hands off the wheel in typical Gallic fashion.

'Anton wishes to make a film about the training of a ballet dancer. He has been reading about your old teacher Olga Valenska and about the big influence she had and he has written a short story about a young girl ... about seventeen ... who joins the ballet school run by an old *prima ballerina* in Paris to finish her training as a classical dancer. The film will cover a couple of days in the life of the girl, showing her going to her classes, covering her relationship with the teacher, the other pupils, her audition at a theatre for a part in a stage musical, her failure to get the part and her return the next day to classes and the same routine of exercise and practice. You get the idea? You still remember what it was like, eh? The ups and the downs, the pain and suffering, the small triumphs?'

'Yes, I do,' Roselle muttered fervently.

'It will be a realistic film, then, but it will be beautiful too, as all Charron's films are, with wonderful visual effects, especially in the dance sequences when the old ballerina is guiding the young dancers through the steps and arm movements, the phrasings necessary for some of the great dancing roles such as Odette in *Swan Lake,* or Giselle. You are beginning to be interested?'

'It sounds wonderful!' As always his enthusiasm was making her enthusiastic too. Already she was imagining scenes from the unmade film. 'Are you going to direct the dance sequences?'

'But of course I am. Why would I be telling you about it if I wasn't? Most of the company will be involved as the ballet class in the story and I am hoping that once he has met you today Anton will choose you to play the role of the young girl.' He gave her a sharp, assessing glance. 'You still look as if you're only seventeen.'

'Thank you,' she retorted primly, making a face at him.

'But I could have wished you were not on crutches for this meeting,' he went on critically as he drove serenely right across the Etoile, in front of several approaching cars, ignoring completely the blare of their horns. 'It is difficult to appear graceful and elegant when you are hobbling about. *Mais c'est la vie.*' He shrugged his slim shoulders and turned right down a long tree-lined boulevard. 'Anton will not, after all, be judging you on your ability to dance—*I'll* do that. He will be watching you this afternoon while you talk, listening to your voice, deciding whether it is possible for him to mould you into the character of the dancer. *Comprends-tu?*'

'Yes. When does he want to make the film?'

'As soon as he has decided on whether you are suitable. He has the rest of the small cast lined up. I expect he'd like you to be available next week to start learning your part and possibly to film any scenes which do not include actual dancing. They can be done when your ankle is better. It will take most of July and August to do the shooting.'

'But I was thinking of going away for a holiday next week,' she said.

'Where? With whom?' The questions were shot at her rapidly.

'I've been invited to go and stay at Cap d'Antibes.'

René swore fluently and flicked her an impatient glance.

'You'll be a fool if you accept that invitation,' he said.

'Why?'

'Because this film could do more to boost your career as a dancer more quickly than any liaison with Adrian Corwell can. What has he offered you? *Carte blanche*? Be his mistress and he will make you a *prima ballerina* with your own company and his financial backing?' he asked scornfully.

'He wants to marry me.'

'*Mon dieu*!' he exploded. 'That's even worse!' He threw up his hands in horror, letting go of the steering wheel, of course, and the car swerved about the road alarmingly. 'Do you think a man like him would ever let you out of his sight to do what you want to do once you're married to him? Ha! He would want to direct your life in the same way he directs his companies. Anyway, marriage for a woman is always a sort of serfdom.'

'I don't agree. It doesn't have to be like that,' Roselle retorted.

'How do you know? You haven't been married yet.'

She looked away from him out at the factories and blocks of apartments they were passing as they drove towards the Porte d'Orléans. She hadn't told René she was married to Léon. It hadn't seemed necessary to tell him when he had asked her to join the company.

'So what are you going to do?' he barked at her.

'Come with me to Barbizon or go back to your apartment to wait around until Adrian comes to take you out to dinner?' Again his scorn seared her. 'It's a good thing we have not left the city yet—' he braked the car suddenly, much to the irritation of the driver of the car behind and ran it close to the curb. 'Decide now,' he rapped. 'Do you want to be in that film? Dancers of your quality are two a penny, you know. I can easily find another to take your place.'

Another decision to make and no one around to whom she could turn for advice. From the past came the memory of Léon saying just before he had left her in London, *'You would be wise to take the opportunity to go on tour. You can come to Montenay another time.* What would he say now if she told him she had a chance to take a part in a film? Wouldn't he tell her to make the most of the situation?'

She turned to René, but he wasn't looking at her. He was staring out of the window on his side of the car and his fingers were tapping an impatient tattoo on the wheel. Roselle knew him well enough now to believe he had meant it when he had said dancers of her quality were two a penny. It hurt to be told that after struggling for so long to do her best, but she supposed she should be grateful for his interest and encouragement.

'Cap d'Antibes would have been nice,' she said with a sigh. 'But I would rather go with you to meet

Anton Charron and take part in that film, even if I don't get the leading role.'

'Aha!' René turned to her with a dazzling smile. He put his hands on her shoulders and kissed her on both cheeks. 'That is more like you. And now let's get on our way.' The car roared out into the traffic again. 'Whew, this heat is terrible! Like being in the Sahara desert. It will be good to get down to the country for a few hours.'

The scenery of the southern part of the Ile de France into which they drove as they left Paris behind was heartwarmingly familiar, immortalised as it has been by scores of French artists, from the time of Corot. In the golden haze of summer they drove along lanes bordered with silvery poplars and through neat grey-stone villages hiding amongst clumps of oak and beech trees. Barbizon was a single street lined with restaurants and hotels for the hundreds of visitors who go there in search of the beauty found there by the artists. As they drove through it René pointed out the houses of Millet and Rousseau which had become small museums.

Anton Charron lived in a small elegant house on the outskirts of the pretty village and he and his wife Hortense entertained Roselle and René to an excellently cooked meal of *coq au vin* and raspberry soufflé on an outdoor terrace overlooking a placid river valley. There was good wine and good conversation and almost before she realised it Roselle was telling Anton about Olga Valenska and her own experiences as a pupil at the elderly ballerina's school.

He was an easy man to talk to, quiet and sleepy-eyed, quite unlike the excitable, volatile René. Occasionally he asked her a well thought out question, but it was not until lunch was over that Roselle realised she had been auditioned for the leading role in the film quite thoroughly.

To her secret elation he offered her the part, and the rest of the afternoon was spent discussing with him and René schedules for the rehearsals and actual filming. Some of the work was to be done in a television studio in Paris and some in an old house which had been rented for the purpose. Other scenes would take place in various points of interest in the capital city.

It was well past four o'clock when René at last drove the Peugeot away from Barbizon and turned north along the road to Paris, but it was still very hot and the sky over the city had an unpleasant coppery sheen, hinting at a storm to come. After making arrangements to see Roselle the next day when he intended to take her to the television studio to start rehearsing her in her speaking part René dropped her off at the building where she lived. In the apartment she found a note on the kitchen table left by Cécile. It stated briefly that Adrian had called and wanted her to phone him when she got in. He would be at the hotel where he usually stayed.

Before phoning Roselle took a bath in lukewarm water in an attempt to cool off. She wound a fresh bandage around her ankle, then dressed in a thin shift-like house coat made from thin Indian cotton embroidered at the neck and at the edges of its wide three-quarter-length sleeves. She hung golden hoops in her ears to glint amongst the reddish-brown waves of her hair and after deciding that she looked a little pale she put some rouge on her cheeks and made up her eyes.

Then she phoned Adrian. The phone in his room at the hotel rang only once before he answered and she had the impression he had been sitting beside it waiting for it to ring. He spoke brusquely.

'I'll come round to your apartment straight away.'

His mood didn't sound too good, she thought with a little grimace as she replaced the receiver, but that was not surprising considering he had driven all the way to Montenay only to find that she wasn't there. In the living room she hobbled around tidying up as best she could. Outside the sky was darkening rapidly as thunder clouds spread across the sky, and as the first lightning flickered she closed the wide sliding window which opened on to the balcony, then switched on the two table lamps.

'You know where I've been, I expect,' Adrian said curtly when she let him in. He was carrying the small suitcase of her clothes which Cécile had given him and he looked his age, his face drawn into severe lines, his pale eyes glinting with a hostile light as their glance took in the crutches on which Roselle was leaning.

'Yes, Cécile told me when I got back here yesterday afternoon,' Roselle replied as he closed the door. He put down the case, but didn't attempt to kiss her as had been his habit lately whenever they met but stood frowning at her, just like an irate parent might frown at an adolescent who puzzled him. 'I told you before I went to Montenay that I would come back,' she explained earnestly as she swung on the crutches towards the couch. 'And I did,' she added as she sat down and raised her legs on to the couch to rest the injured ankle.

Adrian took the crutches from her and leaned them against the end of the couch within her reach. But he did not sit down on the chair she had placed for him near to the couch. Hands thrust into the pockets of his superbly tailored grey suit jacket, he stood over her, still frowning.

'You also said you would come back the same day and that you would phone me that evening. Why didn't you?' he rapped.

'I know I did,' she replied shortly, her own temper beginning to rise as she resented the tone of his questioning. It would be like this if she were married to him, she realised. Every time she went anywhere, every time she did anything which didn't please him she would be subjected to this sort of jealous questioning. As René had so shrewdly remarked, her life wouldn't be her own again. And she knew she couldn't live like that. She had to be free to come and go as she wished. Her spirit craved freedom in the same way that Léon's did. She looked up at Adrian, facing his suspicious stare frankly. 'I forgot,' she said flatly. ' I was so worried about my ankle.'

'I see. And I suppose it never occurred to you that I might be worried too when you hadn't phoned by eleven o'clock. That was why I found out the number at Montenay from the directory enquiry people. I phoned several times before anyone answered. Where the hell were you and Chauvigny? What were you doing?'

'I don't think I have to answer that question,' she retorted coolly, and his eyes narrowed unpleasantly.

'He told me about your injury and said he thought you would probably stay for a while,' he went on. 'And so I thought it would be a good idea if I drove down to pick you up, see him at the same time and make sure that you had asked him about a divorce. Why didn't you stay there, at least until I arrived?'

'Because I wanted to have my ankle examined by Dr Messange. As you know, he treated Anya. He's what we call a "dance" doctor, and understands that an injury to a dancer's legs or feet should not be treated like an injury to a non-dancer's legs or feet. When Léon told you I would probably be staying at Montenay to rest my ankle he didn't know I intended to leave the next day,' she answered calmly. 'But why didn't you stick to your original intention to go there on Friday? Why did you go yesterday? If you hadn't gone you'd have been here when I came back yesterday afternoon.'

'Because I didn't like the idea of you being with him too long,' he said. 'I couldn't get it out of my mind that he might....' He broke off, dull colour staining his face.

'That he might what?'

'That he might ... *God*, how can I put it?' muttered Adrian in a strangely choked voice, passing his hand over his hair in an embarrassed way as he turned and paced away from her towards the window. 'I was afraid he might assert his conjugal rights and then there wouldn't be any chance of you getting an easy annulment of your marriage,' he added in a muffled voice. He swung round to stare at her across the shadowy room. 'Foolish of me, wasn't it?' he grated. 'To be jealous and suspicious like that, so jealous that I cancelled everything on Thursday to drive down there like some knight errant in a tale of romance determined to rescue his lady from the clutches of her evil, lecherous husband. But then it's been said, I believe, that a fool at forty is a fool indeed, and I'm well over forty.'

Muttering something else inaudible, he turned away from her and stared out at the rain which was now streaming down the window pane.

'I don't think you're a fool,' Roselle said quietly.

'Don't you?' He came back across the room to her. 'Yet you're the one who has made a fool of me,'

'How?'

'You led me first of all to believe that you were single and innocent. You've led me a dance for over a year now, ballerina.'

'But not deliberately,' she replied defensively. 'I never asked you to follow me all over Europe.'

'But you didn't tell me once to get lost or to leave you alone,' Adrian retorted. 'Never once did you refuse my invitations to lunch or dine with me, so naturally I thought, or I began to think, you liked me.'

'I did like you ... I do like you, and you made it very difficult for me to refuse your invitations,' she argued in a whisper, remembering how he had persisted, always waiting for her at the stage door of any theatre the company had been performing in, to urge her into a taxi or into his car, never giving her a chance to say she had other plans or wanted to go with her younger friends. 'You can be very overbearing,' she explained. 'And I didn't like to hurt your feelings by refusing. You aren't the first to have pursued me,' She shrugged her shoulders rather fatalistically. 'It's something we women dancers have to put up with and I thought that sooner or later when you found out that I wasn't interested in being your mistress or pillow friend, like the others you would lose interest and stop following me. I ... I ... never expected you to ask me to marry you.'

'I see,' Adrian said again, his breath hissing between his set teeth. 'I pushed you into a corner, did I? So you were forced to admit you were married. I gave you an excuse to go and see your beloved Léon. When did you ask him about a divorce? Before or after you slept with him?' he sneered.

Roselle felt her face go pale with shock. She couldn't have been more shaken if he had slapped her across the face.

'What did Léon say to you? What did he tell you?' she cried. 'Surely he didn't tell you....' She broke off to cover her face with her hands, realising how much she had betrayed herself by her uncontrolled reaction to Adrian's taunt.

'Actually he said very little. When I asked him where you'd gone he asked me what business was it of mine. I told him I wanted to marry you and....' Adrian paused, then added in a voice choked with rage, 'He was damned insolent!'

'Oh, I knew you and he shouldn't meet,' groaned Roselle, lifting her face from her hands. 'What did he say?' she demanded urgently. 'Did he ... did he say he would agree to a divorce?'

'He laughed in my face, said he didn't care for people who poached on his preserves and told me to leave before he threw me out. Then he walked out of the room. Oh, he was very sure of himself, very much the man in possession ... of you.' Again

Adrian drew in a hissing breath. 'Why did you let me believe there's no love between you and him?' he asked in a steadier voice.

'But there isn't, there isn't,' she said wildly. 'He doesn't love me. He married me only because it was arranged by his grandmother. And I ... well, I hate him.'

'Because he doesn't run after you, perhaps,' he suggested wearily. 'But call it what you like, there's something between you two, a sort of invisible bond, and I'm not prepared to try and break it. Even if you were able to get a divorce and you and I did marry, you would always belong to him.' He sighed and rubbed a hand over his face. 'God, I'm tired,' he muttered, and gave her a rather wintry smile. 'That's my age telling. Two sleepless nights in a row and all that driving are too much. Shall we call it a day, Roselle?'

'You're leaving?'

'I'm leaving. I'm getting right out of your life. Forget I asked you to marry me. Forget I invited you to Cap d'Antibes to stay with me and my family. Come to think of it, they're going to be very relieved that I've decided to give you up. My daughter is almost as old as you and might have resented you.'

'And you dare to accuse me of deceiving you because I didn't tell you I was married!' Roselle gasped, staring at him incredulously. 'You never told me you had a daughter. You never told me you'd been married.'

'Twice,' he admitted. 'Both of them failures. I thought the third time might be lucky ... with you. But I can see now I was indulging in a sort of romantic fantasy, enjoying a flare-up of my youth again.' His mouth twisted wryly. 'We've both learned something from the happenings of the past two days and from our little affair, I hope. You'll have learned to say no to middle-aged men when they pester you with their attentions. And I'll have learned that young, gentle, pretty girls like you usually belong already to someone else.' He glanced towards the window. 'I think the storm is over now, so I'll go back to the hotel. I hope your ankle soon gets better. Goodbye, my dear.'

'Goodbye....'

Adrian went out, closing the door behind him. Roselle's shoulders sagged with relief. Her innocent and slightly one-sided extra-marital affair with an older man was over. It had got a little out of hand, she could see that now, but Léon had put an end to it for her.

The door of the apartment opened and Cécile came in. She looked round cautiously.

'Did you get the message I left?' she asked.

'Yes. Adrian has just left—for good this time.'

'So?' Cécile's dark eyes twinkled. 'You have got rid of him at last. And how do you feel about that?'

'Relieved,' said Roselle, and they both laughed together.

'Then you won't be going to Cap d'Antibes for a holiday,' Cécile said.

'No. I'd decided not to go anyway. Cécile, why didn't you tell me we're all going to be in a film about ballet training?'

'I thought it best if René told you himself. Isn't it exciting?' Cécile executed several pirouettes on her way to the kitchen. 'But I think it would be a good idea if you had a proper rest before the filming begins. How would you like to come down to the seaside with me tomorrow? My aunt and uncle keep a small pension at a fishing village on the Breton coast. We could stay there for a few days, loll about on the beach, soak up some sun and fresh air. It won't be luxury like a villa at Antibes. . . .'

'I'd love to come,' said Roselle. 'How do we get there?'

The change was just what she needed to put things in perspective again, and by the end of the six days they spent 'lolling' about on the beach her ankle was much better and she was able to walk about on it without pain. As soon as they returned to Paris she began to exercise cautiously, taking care not to favour the foot that had been damaged too much in case she placed too many extra burdens on the other and ended up with bruised and painful muscles.

Then there was the excitement of taking part in the film. Every day after attending the Ballet Godin's dance studio to do their usual daily class she and Cécile went off to another studio where some of the indoor shots of the film were being made and where they spent the rest of the day usually watching scenery being set up when they weren't being rehearsed by Anton or René.

The part of the girl in the story came easily to Roselle because the story could have been about herself or any one of the other dancers in the company, and she found that the actress who had been chosen to play the part of the ballet teacher so like Olga that acting the story was almost like living a part of her life all over again ... except that there was no Léon in it, no tantalisingly elusive man to torment and entice her.

There was no Léon in her life now, either. Only in her thoughts and her dreams did he exist. She had half expected him to write to her to tell her that he had met Adrian, sized him up and had decided that he wasn't a more suitable husband for her than himself and so he couldn't agree to a divorce. But she heard nothing from him during the first few weeks after Adrian had departed and in the end, unable not to confide in him, she wrote to him telling him how busy she was making the film, how her ankle was better and how classes and rehearsals for the new ballet season would soon be starting up, at the end of August as soon as the film-making had finished. She didn't mention Adrian.

After a while she received one of his polite letters in which he said he was glad to hear her ankle was better, was interested to hear about the film which he hoped he would see one day. He was busy too. The summer had been a good one and soon the grapes would be ready to pick. He was expecting a good vintage this year, possibly one of the best Montenay had ever had, and at last he would be established as a successful *vigneron* whose wines could compete with the best. He did not mention Adrian either. Nor did he say he hoped to see Roselle soon. Nor did he ask her if she was going to visit Montenay again. The letter irritated her by its coolness and after reading it she was tempted to tear it up, but she didn't. She put it carefully away with the other letters she had received from Léon over the years, and it was when she was doing that that she found the copy of the marriage contract they had both signed and, remembering what he had said about the clause concerning her dowry, she took it out and read it.

Yes, it was there in black and white, as he had said it was, written in complicated legal French which she found hard to translate. But she got the gist of it. If for any reason the marriage should break up Léon was to pay back to her the exact amount of money which she would have received from Olga if the original will of the old lady had been in effect when she had died.

This was what Léon had read when he had asked to see the marriage contract. This was what had made him so angry. He couldn't have suggested an annulment of their strange marriage then even if he had wanted to because he couldn't have afforded to pay back the money. So he had made the most of the situation.

'Oh, godmother, godmother,' Roselle muttered to herself as she slid the contract back into its envelope, 'why did you do this to us? Why did you trap us both?'

Olga's last letter was there amongst the few letters of Léon's she had kept and she opened it to read it again, searching for an answer to her question, wondering if there was anything in it she had missed on the first reading, just as she had missed the clause in the contract. Because she hadn't wanted to see it? Because she hadn't wanted to face up to the possibility of a break-up of her marriage to Léon? Probably.

'You may wonder sometimes why I arranged your marriage to my grandson Léon,' Olga had written in her sloping spider scrawl. 'Arranged marriages are traditional in this country as they often were in my country when I was young. I did it for the best to help both of you. I was very worried about Léon. He was becoming hardened and embittered by the way of life he was leading as a mercenary soldier. The chance of him buying back the Chauvigny property could not be ignored. To carry on the tradition of his father's family, to return to the land and do the work he had always wanted to do, would be his salvation, I decided, so I gave him the money he needed to buy it back.

'But I could not ignore your needs, *ma petite*. I had promised your parents I would take care of you in the event of their death—that was my responsibility as your godparent. I knew that once I passed on you would be alone in the world, so I decided that because I could not leave you the money I had intended to leave you in my will I would make Léon responsible for you by arranging your marriage to him. I knew you were in love with him, so that presented no problem. His agreement was a little more difficult to get, so I took advantage of him being ill to persuade him to take part in the ceremony. I hoped and I still hope that he will learn to love you.

'Now I am hoping you understand why I have done this. I realise that the ways of an old woman like me who was brought up with different values and in different traditions may seem a little crazy to you, but it is my love for you both which is the root of my madness.'

Roselle laid the letter down. She did understand now, she thought. Or at least she was beginning to understand now that she knew a little more about love.

But Olga's hopes had not been fulfilled. Although Léon had been able to buy back Montenay and give up the rather questionable career of being a mercenary soldier he had not learned to love her and their marriage had not developed into a proper marriage. They weren't partners and didn't share anything.

She had no more time to think about it that day because she had to go to the dress rehearsal of the new American modern dance ballet which René had decided to put on, with her dancing the leading part of the wife in a story told in mime and dance about, ironically enough, the break-up of a marriage caused by the pressures of modern life.

Outside it was a lovely day, so she went by bus to the small theatre just off the Champs Elysées. The late September sun was warm and mellow and in the Tuileries gardens autumn was a brilliant assortment of colours, purple, bronze, crimson and yellow. The leaves of some of the trees were beginning to turn, taking on tints of gold and copper. At Montenay now the grapes would be fully ripe and the backbreaking job of harvesting them would be in progress.

Unexpectedly Roselle experienced a longing to be there, to work beside Léon in the gold-green vineyard under the blazing sun, to share in his satisfaction because the vintage was a good one, to take part in the wine-making process in the long *chais* building. If only she could be there with him instead of Angèle, joining in the fun and laughter which always accompanied a good vintage. Almost three months had passed since the housekeeper had talked about the fun they all had at the *vendange*. The time had gone by quickly, and yet the summer had seemed too long in spite of all the activity associated with the making of the film. It had been a void during which she had ached to be with Léon.

Perhaps when the vintage was over and the wine had been made he would come to Paris to see her. An idea flashed into her mind. She would find out exactly when the film première would be and would write inviting him to come and see it, to share in her small success. The bus lurched to a stop and looking round she saw she was at the stop near the theatre. As she sprang to her feet and pushed through the people standing on the outside platform of the bus so she could get off, a slight sickness and dizziness swept over her, something which had been happening to her far too often lately for her peace of mind.

Hurrying in the direction of the theatre, she pushed to the back of her mind the niggling suspicion that the sickness was due to the fact that she was pregnant. She ran up the steps to the stage door because she was late. In the dressing room she changed quickly into the simple skirt, blouse and cardigan which she wore as the wife in the ballet. She laced on her *pointe* shoes and made up her face. Her own hair in its normal casual shoulder-length style was suitable, so she flicked a comb through it and then hurried to the stage where René was giving final instructions to the other three dancers who danced in the modern ballet. He gave her a fierce glare to show he was irritated by her lateness, but said nothing, then he snapped his thumb and finger at the pianist and the music began.

It was half way through the trio when Roselle as the wife was dancing with Albert Larson who was playing the part of the husband and they were being watched by Cécile who was dancing the part of their child that Roselle felt the sick giddiness again and was forced to stop dancing to sink down on the stage and put her head between her knees to wait for the dizziness to pass.

René was irritated, but he accepted her apology and the dance continued.

In the second scene of the ballet there was some violently active dancing for both her and Albert to show their disillusionment, and at one time he took hold of her and whirled her round and round. Feeling sickness rising within her, she whispered to him to stop. At once René was up on the stage.

'What is the matter with you?' he demanded angrily.

'I'm sorry—I feel sick and dizzy. If I could just sit down for a while and perhaps have some magnesia or a glass of water it will go away.'

'All right,' he grumbled. 'Clear the stage,' he added to the others. 'We'll have half an hour's break.'

In the dressing room Roselle lay down on an old couch while Cécile fussed over her and some of the other dancers who were waiting about ready to rehearse another ballet crowded round curiously.

Then all scattered like ruffled pigeons when René entered the room carrying a glass of water in which something fizzed slightly.

'Bromo seltzer,' he said. 'It is all I could find. Go and practise,' he ordered Cécile. 'Your miming in the first scene is still sloppy.'

Cécile went out grumbling. René twirled a chair around to straddle it. Arms resting along the back of it, he watched Roselle sip the drink he had brought.

'And now, are you going to tell me what is wrong with you? Do you think I haven't noticed these attacks of dizziness before?' he said in his brisk way. 'Every day you have lost balance at some time during rehearsal. At first I thought it was your partner's fault, but now I know differently. Are you pregnant?'

Roselle stared at him in surprise. He stared back, a slightly mocking expression in his eyes.

'Do you think also I have no experience of this sort of thing?' he queried. 'You aren't the first dancer to become pregnant, you know.'

'I ... I'm not sure. I haven't been to see a doctor yet,' she began.

'You will go tomorrow,' he ordered. 'The most important thing just now is—are you going to be able to perform this evening without flopping to the stage between every scene to put your head between your knees?'

'I want to. I'll be all right ... if we could leave out the part where Albert swings me upside down.'

That's when I feel bad.'

'So I've noticed,' he said dryly. 'All right, we'll leave out the swinging upside down until you are feeling better.' His glance went over her. 'I didn't think you were like some of the other girls,' he drawled. 'I didn't think you slept around.'

'I don't sleep around,' she retorted.

'But you would have to sleep with some man to get pregnant,' he retorted. 'Who was it? Corwell?'

'No, of course not!'

'Don't tell me you have another admirer already,' he scoffed. 'I haven't seen one hanging about, and I've been with you a lot lately.'

That was true. He had been very attentive recently, often taking her back to the apartment after rehearsals. It was something which had begun when the film was being made and her ankle had still been painful to walk on. But she had thought nothing of it, believing his interest in her to be purely professional. After all, she was now a ballerina and to a certain extent they were dependent on each other; she on him for guidance; he on her for good performances which would attract audiences.

But she hesitated to tell him about Léon. In the silence she could hear other dancers laughing and talking in the next room and the slither and soft thudding of feet on the stage above as some of them practised their steps.

'No I don't have another admirer,' she said woodenly.

'And if it is confirmed by the doctor, as I think it will be, that you are going to have a child, what will you do?'

'Do? I ... I don't know. I haven't thought about it yet.'

'*Eh bien*, you had better start thinking,' René rasped, his lips thinning. 'I do not approve of unwanted children being brought into the world. Will you keep it?'

'Of course I will. I couldn't do anything else,' she retorted.

'Why not?'

'Because—oh, because it would be Léon's baby as well as mine and. ...' She broke off, realising she had given herself away.

'And who the hell is Léon?'

'My ... my husband.'

'*Mon dieu*!' He was astounded. 'Why haven't I known this? Why haven't I been told? When did you marry? And where is your husband? Why have I never seen him? Why don't you talk about him all the time like ... like Anya Merimée goes on about her Gilles?'

'Léon and I live separately,' she said stiffly.

'But not all the time, obviously, if you're going to have his child,' he said dryly. '*Mon dieu*,' he muttered again. 'It's incredible! I had thought you were different. I had thought you were totally dedicated to your career, truly professional, putting it before everyone and everything else.' His expression grew bitter. 'I was even beginning to think that perhaps you're the only woman I could relate to. I was even thinking of asking you to live with me.'

'Live with you?' Roselle repeated in bewilderment.

'*Oui*. You know I do not care much for marriage. I regard it as a barbarous invention, a form of slavery for both the man and the woman, a tribal institution. But now....' His angry glance raked her critically. 'Now I find out you are no better than any other of the silly women I've met and you're going to have another man's child....'

'René, please, I'd no idea you....'

'That I was beginning to feel possessive?' he finished for her with a whimsical twist of his wide mobile mouth. 'No, I don't suppose you had. It has come as a surprise to me too.' He gave her a curious glance. 'Are you in love with him? No, don't bother to answer that. You wouldn't want to keep his child if you weren't. What does he do? Why isn't he here in Paris with you?'

She told him then all about her marriage, leaving nothing out as she had when she had told Adrian. When she had finished René stared at her thoughtfully, then said slowly,

'So what is the next step? What will you do next? If it is confirmed by the doctor tomorrow will you tell Léon?'

'I don't know. I'll have to think about it.' Roselle slid off the couch and stood up. 'I feel better now.

Shall we go on with the rehearsal?'

That night the Ballet Godin opened its new season to a gratifyingly full house and the two ballets performed went off without a hitch. The next day there were good if not rave reviews in two of the morning newspapers and Roselle was pleased to see that one of the critics praised her performance in the American ballet as 'delicate and emotionally moving.' She read the reviews while she waited to see the gynaecologist who had been recommended to her.

Later, after spending an hour walking about in a rather stunned way, she went to the theatre to class as usual and told René it was positive; she was going to have a baby.

'But the doctor says there's no reason why I shouldn't go on dancing, at least until the end of November,' she said when she saw his face darken irritably. 'You will let me, won't you?'

'You'll dance for as long as you feel like it,' he said coolly. 'But it will not be in a leading role. I have already asked Carlotta Morin to take your place in the modern dance. I have just been watching her perform. She is good, possibly better than you are, and she has no problems with swinging upside down. You will go back to the *corps de ballet* until after you have had your baby.' He turned away from her and called to the pianist to start playing again.

Feeling sick, not from pregnancy but from disappointment, Roselle watched Carlotta glide on to the stage. The dancer was good. Her mime was perfect as she danced about the stage in a lighthearted way, expressing the happiness of the newly married wife in the story.

Tears welled in Roselle's eyes. How brief her time as ballerina had been! Her chance of fame had come and gone. She had lost it because she had made the mistake of going to see Léon. Never would she go and see him again. Never.

René turned to her abruptly as if sensing her distress.

'Don't cry, Rosie,' he said softly, putting an arm about her shoulders and hugging her. 'You'll have another chance after the baby has been born. Have you decided what to do? Are you going to tell Léon about the child?'

'Not yet. I think I'll wait until after the vintage is over,' she muttered, and freeing herself from his arm she left the auditorium of the theatre to go back stage to the dressing room, to change into the costume she would wear in the next ballet as a member of the *corps de ballet*.

CHAPTER SIX

THE long hot summer came to an end at last, as the golden days of September gave way to the shorter, cooler but equally golden days of October. The leaves in the parks and along the boulevards changed colour completely, withered and died, to be blown away by the wind and rain which brought in November.

And as the weeks went by Roselle felt her body changing slowly and inevitably until one morning she felt movement, faint but sudden, like the delicate shaking of a bird's wing, and in that instant all her resentment towards her pregnancy faded, lost in the sudden surge of exhilaration which she felt because she was going to be a mother.

It was that day she told René she intended to stop dancing until after the baby was born. He accepted her resignation with obvious relief, then barked a sharp question at her.

'Have you told Léon yet?'

'No.'

'Why not? You said after the vintage, and that

should be over by now.'

'I know, but . . . oh, it's difficult.'

'Why, for God's sake? The man has a right to know that his wife is going to have his child. And who is going to take care of you?'

'I'll take care of myself,' she retorted coolly, and walked out without further explanation because it was impossible for her to tell him why she couldn't tell Léon.

A few days later, after visiting the doctor for a regular antenatal check-up, she returned to the single ground floor apartment to which she had moved a few weeks previously. She had moved out of the apartment she had shared with Cécile because she had been unable to get enough sleep there. Her new abode was in one of the quieter lesser known areas of Paris, in the southern part of the city, off the tourist track.

It was raining steadily when she got off the bus and darkness was setting in. She called at the bakery at the corner of the street to buy bread and clutching the long loaf, shielding it from the rain with her umbrella, she hurried along the narrow street where old-fashioned gas lights were reflected in the puddles of the pavement.

She reached the tall, flat-fronted grey house where she lived, paused on the door step to shake her umbrella and close it, then pushed open one of the narrow double doors and stepped into the hallway. She turned towards the *concierge*'s office and her heart stood still when she saw the man who was leaning in the office doorway talking to Madame Duchène, the *concierge*.

'Léon!' she gasped.

'*Bonjour*, Roselle,' he said coolly. 'How are you?'

'Well, thank you,' she whispered, unable to stop staring at him. Then the walls seemed to be leaning in on her and the floor seemed to be coming up towards her. She heard Madame Duchène's shrill exclamation of concern. But she didn't fall because strong arms were around her holding her up. They lifted her and carried her. Her cheek was against the dampness of a leather coat and she felt safe, very, very safe.

Into her apartment Léon carried her, through the door hastily opened by the *concierge*. Down on the old chesterfield he laid her, carefully. Everything stopped whirling about her and she saw the *concierge* hovering behind him curiously.

'It's all right, Madame Duchène,' she whispered. 'Monsieur Chauvigny is my husband.'

The woman gave Léon a suspicious glance which he returned with one of his rare yet radiantly boyish grins.

'You think perhaps we do not behave like husband and wife?' he challenged her. 'But I assure you, *madame*, it is true. We are married.'

Madame Duchène capitulated at once. Her face softened and she nearly smiled.

'Very well, *monsieur*. I believe you.' She glanced

anxiously at Roselle. 'But you, *made* ... I mean *madame*, you do not seem well. You had a shock at the door just now and that is not good when one is *enceinte*....'

'I'm all right, thank you,' Roselle interrupted her quickly as she noticed Léon's dark glance swerve to her face enquiringly.

'So.' The woman shrugged her shoulders fatalistically. 'Whatever you say.'

She went from the room, closing the door behind her. Léon slipped off his leather jacket, the same one he had worn nearly three years ago when he had come to see Roselle in London, she noticed. As then he was wearing black, a smooth cotton shirt taut across his shoulders and chest with shiny white pearl buttons down at the front and at the cuffs and well-cut black pants belted at the waist and hugging his hips. He threw his coat down across a chair and, turning, came back to her, loosening the knot of the grey and red tie he was wearing and slipping undone the collar button of his shirt as if he resented its confinement.

'How do you feel now?' he asked, his dark glance flicking over her and seeming to her to linger curiously on her waistline and her stomach. 'Can I get you anything?'

'A ... a glass of water, please. You'll find a glass in the cupboard in the kitchenette.'

He went away into the smaller room and Roselle swung her legs down off the chesterfield and stood up. Her heart was still beating a little erratically, but she felt quite steady otherwise. She took off her raincoat and hung it up behind the door, looked around and found her loaf of bread and was just taking it into the kitchenette when Léon came out carrying the glass of water. She took it from him and gave him the bread, which he took into the kitchen. When he appeared again she was sitting in the only armchair, her feet on a small footstool, and was sipping the water. He switched on a lamp, pulled the curtains across the window and came back to sit down on the chesterfield.

'I'm sorry I don't have any wine,' she apologised.

'It doesn't matter,' he said, leaning back and looking round the room. 'How long have you been living here?'

'Nearly a month.'

'Why didn't you write and tell me you had changed your address?' he asked coolly, and she couldn't tell from his tone of voice or by the expression on his face whether he was annoyed or not because she hadn't told him she had moved.

'I ... don't know,' she mumbled evasively.

'Hiding?' he challenged, and she looked at him swiftly and warily.

'From whom?' she countered.

'From me?'

'Why should I want to hide from anyone?' she parried uneasily. 'Anyway, how did you find out I lived here?'

'I called at the other address. Your former apartment mate was just leaving for the theatre to rehearse. She wasn't going to give me this address.' One corner of his mouth slanted upwards and his eyes were veiled by their lashes. 'But she soon broke under pressure,' he drawled. 'If she hadn't I'd have followed her to the theatre and found out from someone there, perhaps.' His glance flicked up to her face again. 'She says you don't dance very much these days. I am sorry for that. I had hoped to watch you. What about the film you told me about in your last letter? Has it been shown yet?'

'No, not yet.' Roselle felt tense, as if she were sitting on the edge of a precipice. Hadn't Léon heard what Madame Duchène had said about her being pregnant after all? 'It's still being edited. But René says it might be ready for showing next month.'

'René?' he queried.

'The director of the Ballet Godin.' She paused, then added in a rush, determined to get him away from the subject of herself, 'Was the vintage up to your expectations?'

'*Oui*, it was very good. The wine is made now and I was able to enter some litres of it for auction at Beaune during Les Trois Glorieuses.'

'What's that?' she asked quickly.

'The Three Glorious Days when the wines of Burgundy are celebrated. It is a festival when there are

private and public tastings of wine, parades, folk
dancing, six-hour lunches, candlelight banquets....'
Léon stopped, shook his head and laughed. 'I have
just come from it and I am still suffering from a
hangover.'

'Did anyone buy your wine at the auction?'

'*Mais oui*. It fetched a good price. The auction is
a great publicity show as well as being the greatest
charity sale in the world because the proceeds from
the sale of the wine go to the support of the old
hospital in Beaune. It is a way for a new *vigneron*
like myself to become known and for the wine which
I have produced to be tasted and receive approval
from expert tasters and merchants. One of the
tasters, Henri Patinot, said this year's product from
Château Montenay could hold its place with a Montenay wine which was made in 1929. As a result I
was able to sell the rest of it at a good profit.' He
gave her a level look, 'So you see, *ma mie*, I am now
in a position to agree to a divorce if you still want
one. I can afford to pay back the money which
Grand'mère gave me and which should have been
left to you.'

It was the last thing Roselle had expected him to
say and it chilled her to the marrow. She sat as if
turned to stone, staring at him.

'Roselle.' he leaned forward, 'you are very pale.
Is it true what the *concierge* said, just now? Are you
expecting a baby?'

'Yes, it's true,' she whispered. Her eyes feasted

greedily on the amber-streaked hair falling forward over his forehead, on the almost oriental slant of his almost black eyes, on the tough angles and lines of his cheeks and jaw, on the provocative curve of his mouth, somehow emphasized by the dark blur of moustache and beard stubble which indicated that as always he would have to shave for a second time that day. He had come as she had hoped he would, without her having to ask him to come. He had only been in the room ten minutes and already she was affected by his animal-like grace, the suggestion of moodiness in his face, by the mystery that was him.

'How long?' he asked laconically.

'About five months.'

His eyes narrowed fractionally as he calculated.

'So it could be mine,' he said, his glance not shifting away from her eyes, no smile softening his mouth.

'It is yours,' she flared suddenly. 'Oh, how can you believe otherwise?'

'Because last time I saw you you were on very friendly terms with a certain Adrian Corwell,' he retorted. 'And you were wanting a divorce so you could be free to accept his proposal of marriage.' He glanced round the room, his mouth curling in distaste at its shabbiness. 'I admit this is not the sort of place I would have expected a man of his affluence to rent for his mistress, but....' He made a gesture with his hands and shrugged, his glance coming back to her, stabbing her with its sudden bright penetration. 'The child could also be his.'

'It could not!' she seethed furiously. She was out of her chair in one quick movement and was standing over him, her hands clenched at her side. 'I haven't seen Adrian since he came back from Montenay. He changed his mind about wanting to marry me—or rather you changed it for him.'

'I did?' Léon tipped his head back lazily against the back of the chesterfield. 'How did I do that?'

'You said you didn't like people who poached on your preserves and threatened to throw him out if he didn't leave.'

'Mmm. Must have lost my temper, mustn't I?' he drawled, his glance sliding down over her suggestively. 'I wonder why?' He lifted a hand suddenly, grasped one of her wrists and before she had a chance to twist free he had her down on the chesterfield beside him and was leaning over her threateningly. 'If this baby is mine,' he said softly, and slid a hand insolently over her waist and stomach, 'why have you not told me about it? Why have you kept it to yourself? Are you ashamed of it because it is mine? Were you hoping to get rid of it?'

'No, no!' She was horrified by what he was suggesting. 'Oh, how can you say such things? How can you even think them? And why have you come here? To torment me?'

With her free hand she beat at him, anywhere she

could hit him, on the shoulders and on the chest. Letting go of her wrist, he put both arms about her and pulled her against him, holding her tightly so that she couldn't move, and she broke then, gave way to the emotions she had been bottling up for the past few weeks, sobbing and snuffling into his shoulder. When she stopped eventually from sheer exhaustion and could only lie limply against him as he continued to hold her, although not so tightly.

'I have come because I wanted to see you,' he said softly after a while. 'I couldn't come before because the wine had to be made and sold. It has been bad for you the last few months, eh?' With a hand under her chin he lifted her face from his shoulder so he could look at her.

'Yes,' she whispered, knuckling a few stray tears away from her eyes.

'For me, too,' he murmured. 'It was too long a summer for both of us, but it is over now and we can be together again for a while.'

'Together? Where?' she asked, pushing away from him.

'At Montenay. You're coming back with me. You'll be better off there in your condition than in this place.' He made a dismissing gesture at the room. 'You'll have good food and fresh air. The child can be born there, and since you are so sure it is mine, can grow up there.'

He was doing what she hadn't wanted him to do. He was taking the responsibility—not because he loved her but because he was married to her, tied to her in an arranged marriage which he could now afford to untie.

'I'm not going with you to Montenay,' she retorted stubbornly.

'Why not?'

'Because I know you're only asking me to go with you because you feel responsible.'

'*C'est vrai*.' A faintly mischievous smile curved his mouth. 'When you came to see me in June I was so excited at seeing you again I didn't take any precautions. You have that effect on me, *ma chérie*.' He leaned towards her until his lips were only an inch or two from hers. 'You are having it now,' he whispered, and the heavy-lidded sultry expression was in his eyes. '*Tu m'enivres* always.'

'No, you mustn't,' she said urgently, although her lips were already quivering in response to the kiss which they had not received. She shifted away from him along the couch, moving to safety, as she thought. 'I don't want you to feel responsible for me. I can take care of myself. And I know you don't really want me at Montenay. You wish you weren't married to me like ... like you wished you weren't when you came to London.'

A quick frown darkened his face and the expression in his eyes became wary, and Roselle knew she had hit on a truth.

'You see, I know now why you were so angry when you read the marriage contract,' she went on breathlessly. 'You visited me in London in the hope of annulling the marriage, didn't you?'

Eyes suddenly blank and expressionless, Léon studied her face for a few seconds before replying.

'I admit it,' he said with a shrug. 'But that was before. . . .'

'And just now you asked me if I still wanted a divorce,' she rushed on, interrupting him. 'Well, the answer is yes, I do. You don't have to stay married to me any more if you don't want to ... just because I'm going to have your child.'

She felt very pleased with the way she had spoken. Her voice hadn't shaken once. She had been able to look him straight in the eyes and show him how independent of him she could be.

'Bravo,' he mocked quietly. 'You act well, *chérie.*'

'I'm not acting,' she flared. 'I mean every word I say!'

'*Vraiment?*' His eyebrows went up in scepticism. 'Then let me say something to you that I mean too,' he retorted autocratically. 'There will be no more talk of divorce.'

'But you said. . . .'

'Will you be quiet!' he snarled, his lips thinning, his eyes glinting angrily. 'We are going to stay married until after our child is born—and it will be born at Montenay where you will live with me for as long as necessary. Now go and start packing your clothes while I ask the *concierge* to call a taxi to take us to the station.'

'I'm not going with you and there's nothing you can do to make me,' Roselle countered, tilting her chin at him defiantly.

'You think not?' Léon drawled silkily, his eyes narrowing to two dark slits of devilment as he pulled undone the knot of his tie and began to flick undone the buttons down the front of his shirt. He leaned towards her again, pushing her into the corner of the couch, his arm stretching in front of her to prevent her escape. 'I think there is,' he went on, his breath warm against her cheek. 'And I don't really know why I didn't do it before. I suppose I was too concerned about the state of your health. But it seems you are in very good health after all, and your pregnancy is not so far on that you can't. . . .'

'No, Léon, you're not to!' she cried as his hand slid round to the nape of her neck. 'I won't let you. I won't!' She put out urgent hands to fend him off, but as soon as they touched his chest and felt the hair-crisped skin they turned traitor on her and began to slide under the edge of his shirt. 'Oh, you're always so unfair,' she accused softly.

His lips took possession of hers easily, moving gently yet expertly, coaxing her to respond, which she did wholeheartedly, parting her lips to the flicker of his because this was really what she had been wanting him to do, what she had been aching for him to do for five whole months.

And when he lifted her and carried her into the

small bedroom she didn't hit out at him or ask him to let her go, because to lie close to him on the narrow bed while he smoothed away her clothes was to come alive again.

Under her seeking hands his skin was like supple velvet, warm, tanned by the Burgundian sun. There was mischief and tender mockery in his lips which visited the special, vulnerable hollows of her throat, but passion flared smokily in his heavily-lidded eyes as they appraised her shape and it throbbed like muted cellos in the softness of his voice when with a groan he gathered her against him so closely there was nothing between them.

'If you knew how much I've wanted you all summer long you wouldn't believe I don't really want you at Montenay,' he whispered shakily against her throat. 'I've wanted you there. I wanted you to stay in June. I want you now and you want me. I can tell by the way you are sighing, by the way you are touching me. You've lost control, haven't you, *ma petite*? And so have I. You intoxicate me more than the wine did during *Les Trois Glorieuses*. I am drunk with the taste of your kisses and the feel of your softness against me, and I don't think I can wait much longer....'

Nor could she hold out against him any longer, and as the tides of their passion for each other met and swirled together in ecstatic union she seemed to drown in a flood of sensuousness, only surfacing to lie close against him in hazy contentment. She offered no more reasons for not going back to Montenay with him, knowing he would not believe them if she did after her complete capitulation to his love-making this evening. She would go and live with him, taking each day as it came, because she knew now he was the only man in her life who mattered. He was the man in possession not only of her body but also of her soul.

They did not go to Montenay that evening but left early next morning on the *rapide* for Dijon. From the Burgundian capital they drove to Montenay in the new estate car Léon had bought, and they did not talk much. There seemed to be no need for words, although Roselle acknowledged to herself ruefully that there were still many matters which should be discussed. She had still to be convinced that he wasn't making the most of a situation and using her physical commitment to him purely for his own gratification.

In the pale November sunshine the walls of the Château glowed pastel pink. White cattle still grazed the green slopes below it, but the vines were stripped bare of their leaves and of the plump juicy grapes from which the famous wine of Montenay had always been crushed. The leaves of creeper tumbling over the protective wall surrounding the old house shimmered russet red and the roofing tiles on the long *chais* where the wine had been made and was stored flamed orange against the blue of the sky. In the courtyard late roses bloomed amongst tiny yellow chrysanthemums.

Although she had a feeling of having come home Roselle grew tense as they entered the house, half expecting Angèle to come bouncing into the hallway to greet them. But no one came. The house was quiet and in the faded blue and grey *salon* dust lay thick on the antique furniture. There were no arrangements of flowers on the hearth. The room looked neglected, and as she wandered about while Léon poured wine for them both she felt an urge to set to and clean house.

'Everything is very dusty,' she commented when he came over to her and handed her a glass of red wine.

'I know. I haven't had much time to spare for housework,' he replied, clinking his glass against hers. 'To us and the future,' he added softly, his eyes very bright and demanding. 'You will drink to that today, *ma chérie*,' he ordered.

'To us and the future,' she repeated coolly, and sipped some wine. 'Where is Angèle? Doesn't she keep house for you any more?'

'No. She left soon after you did, in June,' he replied cryptically.

Roselle sat down on the pretty brocade-covered couch where she had sat that hot afternoon at the beginning of the summer.

'So now I know why you wanted me to come here,' she teased him. 'You want me to keep house for you in her place.'

'I would like you to keep house, that is true, but I don't expect you to look after it by yourself,' he replied, sitting down on the footstool at her feet. 'Madame Noblet, the mother of one of the men who works in the vineyard for me, has agreed to come and do some of the heavy cleaning.' He studied the wine in his glass, then gave her a strangely wary glance. 'I am hoping you will take an interest in the house, decide how it should be renovated. There are many alterations still required. For instance, we shall need a room for the child.' His glance grew challenging and Roselle was reminded of the day-dream she had had five months ago when she had lain in the big four-poster bed upstairs. It seemed it could come true—and yet she was still nagged by the feeling that while Léon possessed her she did not and would never possess him.

'Why did Angèle leave?' she asked, returning to another problem which had always bothered her.

'I told her to get out and not come back,' he replied tautly.

'Why? Wasn't she doing her job properly?'

'She was doing it too damned well,' he said between his teeth, and tossing off the wine in his glass he stood up and went to pour some more. 'She seemed to think herself indispensable because she cleaned and cooked for me, She also believed she could interfere in my relationship with you,' he added. 'I was very angry when I found out she had driven you to Tournus that day, on two counts. She had helped you to leave when I wanted you to stay, and she had no right to drive that truck because she had no driving licence.'

'But you shouldn't have been angry with her for helping me. I asked her to help me,' she retorted.

He gave her one of his murderous glinting glances.

'I was angry with you too, make no mistake about that,' he grated. 'And then when that ... that dried-up stick of a man Corwell turned up in the afternoon and had the nerve to insist I tell him where you were because he was going to marry you I let fly. *God*, he was presumptuous!' He drank some more wine. 'It's a good thing he left fast,' he growled. 'He was very close to having his throat slit. I could have slit yours too for daring to prefer him to me....'

'I didn't prefer him to you,' she exclaimed hastily, appalled by the savagery with which he spoke and yet, in a way, elated by it. He was jealous, and if he was jealous surely that meant he cared for her more than he would admit.

'Then why did you say you wanted a divorce so you could consider his proposal of marriage?' he demanded, setting down his half full glass and coming across to tower over her threateningly. 'There must have been something about him you liked. Perhaps it was his money, eh?' he added jeeringly.

'No, it wasn't.' she flared, stung by the jeer. 'I liked him because ... oh, because ... he put me first, made me feel special ... He loved me.'

'And I don't. Isn't that what you're implying ... as usual?' he challenged her.

'Yes, I am.'

Léon stared at her for a moment, his eyes glinting menacingly, then he swung round and strode towards the door.

'Léon, where are you going?' she asked anxiously.

'To fetch Madame Noblet,' he said over his shoulder, and went out.

Roselle was tempted to go after him to continue the argument and did, in fact, get to her feet and start towards the door, only to pause and hesitate when she heard the sound of the estate car starting up.

She had given him a chance to declare his love for her, had tried to goad him into saying it, but he had withdrawn as usual, had avoided commitment. Sighing, she looked around the faded pretty room, thinking of how she would renovate it. She wouldn't change much because she didn't believe in destroying what was old and beautiful just to bring something up to date. It would be necessary to go slowly, to preserve the essential antique quality of the house while making it more comfortable according to present-day standards.

But thinking about it, planning it would give her something to do while she was waiting for the birth of the baby.

Slowly she wandered from room to room on the

ground floor and then upstairs to the bedroom where she had slept when she had visited the Château in June. The room was untidy. The bed unmade, clothes scattered everywhere. Roselle stripped the bed, found clean sheets and remade it. She gathered up the discarded shirts and working pants and went on to examine the room next door. It was also big and airy and had a communicating door to the other room. It would be ideal as a nursery.

She explored all the second floor of the house and was just going downstairs with her arms full of Léon's dirty clothes and the sheets from the bed when he came into the hallway calling her name. Behind him came a short, sturdy grey-haired woman who was dressed in a neat print overall which she wore over a dark skirt and a knitted sweater.

'This is Madame Noblet,' Léon said abruptly, and turning to the woman added, 'My wife will tell you what she would like done in the house this afternoon.'

Madame Noblet nodded shyly at Roselle and wished her good day. Roselle answered her absently, realising that Léon was going out again. Muttering an excuse to the woman, she hurried after him down the passageway to the back entrance of the house.

'Léon, wait! I'd like to talk to you about the....'

'Later. I'll see you later. There are things I have to attend to outside,' he said brusquely, swinging open the door. 'Just as there are things for you to attend to inside,' he added.

'Yes, but.... Aren't you afraid I'll leave again?' she taunted, having to goad him somehow because he seemed to have lost interest in her again.

His reply was to give her another hostile glance before going outside and banging the door closed.

'Madame Chauvigny,' Madame Noblet was behind her, 'would you like me to start work in the kitchen? I noticed that the floor in there needs scrubbing and there are many dishes which need washing before a meal can be prepared.'

'Yes, yes, of course.' Roselle made an effort to control herself. She was the wife of *le patron* and must learn to behave as such, to show she could manage a house as big as this one without running after her husband every few minutes to demand his attention, so she followed Madame Noblet into the big kitchen and they discussed the work which had to be done there. Then she returned upstairs taking with her the necessary cloths and polish to clean the bedroom and the adjoining bathroom.

It was dark before Léon returned to the house and Madame Noblet had left to go back to the village with her son. Roselle had set the kitchen table for the evening meal. She had decided that the dining room was in too decrepit a state for Léon and her to eat in it.

She arranged a bowl of flowers in the middle of the long plain table which was made from rough wood and had found some candles and two silver candlesticks to decorate it with. Pleased with her efforts to make the kitchen look welcoming, she changed into a long evening gown of dark green wool and an amber-coloured blouse of sheer nylon chiffon which had full bishop sleeves and a deeply plunging neckline. She hung her favourite golden hoops in her ears and made up her face. She was ready to greet her husband when he came in from his work and to serve the rich Burgundian beef stew which Madame Noblet had taught her to make that afternoon. And she had to admit she was looking forward to having a meal alone with Léon and to telling him about her plans for renovating the Château.

But he was not alone when he came. He brought with him a thick-set, red-faced, blue-eyed man of about his own age whom he introduced as the local veterinary surgeon, who had been called in that afternoon to attend to the prizewinning Charollais bull which had become sick while Léon had been away in Beaune and Paris. The vet's name was Jaques Leroy. He looked surprised when he was introduced to Roselle and all the time he was drinking the wine which Léon offered him his glance kept straying in her direction.

Half an hour later he was still there drinking wine and talking with Léon and, afraid that the stew might be spoiling, hoping that he might take the hint and leave, Roselle invited him to stay and share the meal with them. To her dismay he accepted the invitation with alacrity. He was a bachelor, he said, and there was no rush for him to get home. He had no pretty wife waiting for him to return, like some people he knew, he added in his jocular fashion, and winked at Léon.

He stayed for the rest of the evening. Roselle did her best to be pleasant to him, trying to appear interested when he talked about various adventures he had had when attending to animals on local farms, but all the time she was wishing Léon would not give him any more wine to drink, because the more he drank the more he talked and the longer he stayed.

In the end, at ten o'clock she had to excuse herself because she felt so tired after her housework. She said goodnight to them both and went upstairs to the ivory and wine-red bedroom. After washing herself and dressing in one of the new voluminous nightgowns she had bought to wear during her pregnancy, she lay in bed watching the moonlight begin to trickle into the bedroom around the edge of the window, trying hard to stay awake until Léon came, but, inevitably, soothed by the country quietness of the house, she fell asleep.

She came awake later disturbed by moonlight slanting directly on to her face. From the deep shadows of the room came the stealthy movements of someone undressing.

'Léon?' she queried.

'Who else?' he countered, sliding into bed beside her. 'Were you expecting the vet?'

She tensed in reaction to suggestion. The hostility and the resentment were still there like a blank wall blocking off any softer feelings he might have.

'Of course not,' she retorted. 'Why should I?'

'You were doing your best to lead him on all evening,' he growled. He hadn't moved into the centre of the bed to be close to her as he usually did when he slept with her but lay on the other side, flat on his back.

'I ... I was not leading him on!' she spluttered. Oh, how could you think I was?'

'You were very pleasant to him, smiling and asking him questions. Why the hell did you ask him to stay for supper?'

'Well, why did you invite him in in the first place?' she countered furiously.

'Because it's the custom to offer a glass of wine to anyone like him on whose services I depend. I never know when I'll have to ask him to come out in the middle of the night to attend to a beast which is in pain.'

'That's what I thought,' she shot back at him. 'And that's the only reason why I was pleasant to him. I ... I asked him to stay for supper because I didn't want your meal to spoil. I hoped he would have the manners to leave then. How you could think I was flirting with him, I don't know.'

'You weren't watching. I was,' Léon retorted dryly. 'Every time you moved his eyes followed you. He was mentally undressing you and bedding you ...'

'Léon, stop it!' she hissed, rearing up in bed and leaning over to glare at him. In the moonlight she saw the dark eyes swerve warily in her direction. 'You weren't ... you can't be jealous!' she gasped incredulously. 'Not of a man I met for the first time tonight?'

He reached out an arm, grasped the frilled, primly buttoned-up front of her nightgown and pulled her down on top of him so that her face was almost touching his.

'Yes, I'm jealous,' he said between set teeth, 'And if I ever see you making up to another man like you were making up to the vet tonight I won't be answerable for what I'll do to him.'

'Don't you think you're being unreasonable and spiteful?' she said, making no effort to get away from him because the feel of his warm muscular body beneath her was penetrating the folds of her nightgown and causing her bones to melt. 'As well as possessive. Just because I'm your wife it doesn't mean you own me,' she went on tauntingly.

'So, you're getting your revenge, are you?' he retorted, his grasp slackening on her nightgown, his fingers going exploring over her breasts. 'You're getting your own back for what I said to you once. All right, I admit it. Ever since you came to visit me in June I've felt possessive about you. Would you like to know why?'

'Yes, please.' Still lying on top of him, Roselle laid her cheek against his, her body moulding itself to his shape.

'*Je pense que je t'aime,*' Léon whispered, and tickled her ear with his tongue. 'I think that I love you.'

'You ... you're not sure?' Her voice quivered, but she lay still holding her breath because at last he was saying what she had wanted to hear him say. Or at least, he had almost said what she had wanted to hear. Apparently he still had a few reservations about committing himself verbally.

'How can I be sure when I don't know what you mean when you talk about love?' he grumbled, pushing her over on to her side so that he could turn and face her. 'All I know is that when you came in June I found I liked being with you more than any other woman I have known and I wanted you to stay and live with me always.'

'But I don't understand. If you felt like that why did you say yesterday you would agree to a divorce if I wanted one?'

Léon was silent for a few moments, stroking her hair, and she could see in the moonlight a frown creasing his forehead as he struggled to make sense of his actions.

'After you had suggested a divorce I thought about it for a long time, all summer in fact,' he said slowly. 'And I decided it might not be a bad idea to put an end to Olga's arrangement, to untie the knot which kept us bound to each other. It wasn't the first time I'd considered it, as you know. But this time I was considering it for a different reason. You see, I've never been able to decide whether what I feel for you is merely the result of being married to you, so I thought if I became unmarried to you I might find out the truth of my own feelings for you. Do you understand what I am trying to say, *ma mie*?'

'I think so.'

'But then when I saw you again yesterday I knew I couldn't go through with it, even though I told you I would agree to a divorce. The fact that you're pregnant gave me a good reason to withdraw my offer, I found I couldn't bear the idea of you being free to marry some other man and I was afraid that if we were divorced I might not be able to get you back. I would rather be tied to you in an arranged marriage than not be married to you at all.' He paused again and stroked the line of her jaw with gentle fingers. 'Do you think it's possible that I love you?' he whispered.

'It sounds as if you might be,' Roselle replied cautiously, touched to the heart by his uncertainty.

'But what about you? When you were here in June you said you didn't love me any more,' he said. 'I didn't believe you at the time, but the next day I began to realise you might mean it when you told me about Corwell and left here in spite of my request that you should stay.'

'In June I thought I was safe,' she confessed, sliding her hands up over his chest and about his neck. 'But after being with you I longed all summer to be with you again.'

'Then why didn't you come back?'

'I couldn't because I believed you didn't love me. That's why I never came to Montenay in the past. I thought you just put up with me because there wasn't anything you could do to change the arrangement. And when I found out the baby was on its way I couldn't tell you because ... I ... I was afraid you might think I was saying I was pregnant to trap you into staying married to me.'

'And all the time I was thinking you didn't stay here in June and that you didn't return because you preferred Corwell to me and were living with him in Paris.' Léon buried his face in the curve between her shoulder and her throat and she felt the warmth of his mouth against her skin and the flutter of his eyelashes. 'It was too long a summer,' he muttered. 'I went through hell.'

'I did too,' she sighed, ruffling his hair.

'So we could say we shared something at last,' he said dryly, raising his head so he could look at her again. 'You know, *ma chérie*, when I get used to this "love" business I think I might love you very much, so much that when the spring comes and the baby has been born I might be able to let you go back to Paris to dance, if you want to ... that is as long as you promise to come back here often to share my bed, this house, the child and everything we own.'

'And I think that by that time I might love you so much I won't want to leave you,' Roselle whispered shakily, awed by the extent of his commitment. It was much more than she had ever hoped for.

'*Eh bien*,' said Léon with a little laugh as he pulled her head against his shoulder and they settled into the position in which they usually went to sleep when they shared a bed. 'It seems that Olga Valenska's arrangement is going to work out after all.'

'Yes, it's going to work out,' said Roselle with a sigh of contentment as she snuggled against him, and as she drifted into sleep she said a silent thank you to the old lady who had loved them both so much she had dared to arrange their marriage.

What the press says about Harlequin romance fiction...

"...light entertainment well-larded with enlightenment.... Romance is a grand concept, an important part of life."
— *Eagle*, Lawrence (Mass.)

"The most popular reading matter of American women today."
— *The Detroit News*

"Women have come to trust these stories about contemporary people, set in exciting foreign places."
— *Best Sellers*, New York

"Harlequin novels have a vast and loyal readership."
— *Toronto Star*

**Harlequin brings you
a book to cherish …**

three stories of
love and romance
by one of your
favorite
Harlequin authors …

JOY
ROMANCE
LOVE

Harlequin Omnibus
THREE love stories in ONE beautiful volume

The joys of being in love...
the wonder of romance...
the happiness that true love brings...

Now yours in the HARLEQUIN OMNIBUS
edition every month wherever
paperbacks are sold.

Harlequin Presents...

The books that let you escape into the wonderful world of romance! Trips to exotic places...interesting plots...meeting memorable people... the excitement of love.... These are integral parts of Harlequin Presents— the heartwarming novels read by women everywhere.

Many early issues are now available. Choose from this great selection!